The Lusts
Of The Lib

velvet

THE LUSTS OF THE LIBERTINES
The Marquis de Sade, 1785
First published as part of:
The 120 Days Of Sodom
ISBN 1 871592 59 3
A Velvet Book
Edited and translated by
Julian Jones, 1997

First edition 1997

Published by
VELVET PUBLICATIONS
83 Clerkenwell Road
London EC1, UK
Tel: 0171-430-9878
Fax: 0171-242-5527
A Bondagebest Production
♦
Design:
Bradley Davis, PCP International
Cover photo:
"Baby Doll 69", © Peter Whitehead 1996

The Lusts Of The Libertines

The Marquis de Sade

CONTENTS

FOREWORD

The 120 Days Of Sodom is often regarded as the Marquis de Sade's core work, containing all the unflinching lusts and cruelties for which he is renowned, with the minimum of philosophical or political counterpoints. Yet within this sprawling, incomplete tract lies another, even more minimal nucleus of pathological perversion: the 447 "complex, criminal and murderous lusts" of the libertines.

These comprise, quite simply, three sections in which de Sade allows his imagination complete freedom to catalogue the wildest depravities and atrocities he can conceive, from incest and coprophilia through to mutilation, torture and bloody murder. Briefly described – he intended to flesh each one out at a later date – these numbered lists achieve a maniacal intensity unsurpassed in the annals of transgressive literature.

In naming the sections, I have emulated the Italian film maker Pier Paolo Pasolini, who gave structure to his film adaptation, *Salo*, by borrowing Dantë's device of the Circles of Hell. Beyond that, the lusts and manias speak for themselves in their profound, often terrifying scope and ingenuity.

The result is pure, undiluted de Sade.

—Julian Jones

ONE

The Circle Of Excrement

act he fondles the pair's buttocks. First the valet's, then the girl's. He finally ejaculates over the valet's arse.

8. This libertine wishes to deflower a girl destined to be married the following day.

9. This libertine wishes a marriage to be performed, and to deflower the bride some time between the ceremony and the moment the couple retire to the conjugal bed.

10. This libertine would have his valet, a very wily character, marry girls left and right and bring them all to his master, who fucks them then sells them as whores to a procuress.

11. This libertine seeks two virgin sisters; he deflowers both of them.

12. He marries a girl, deflowers her, then reveals all is a fraud; once he's fucked her, he abandons her.

13. This libertine will only fuck a maid, and then only straight after another man has deflowered her while he watches. Her cunt must be clotted with fresh spunk.

14. This libertine deflowers maidens with a large dildo then, without penetrating, shoots his spunk into the raw hole he has bored out.

15. This libertine will tolerate none but maids of rank and distinction, paying for them in accordance with their wealth. He has deflowered more than fifteen hundred of them over a period of thirty years.

16. This libertine forces a brother to fuck his sister while he watches, then fucks the sister himself. He obliges both to shit beforehand.

17. He forces a father to fuck his daughter, once he himself has ruptured her maidenhead.

18.

19. This libertine must have virgins between the age of thirty and forty to deflower.

20. This libertine will only deflower nuns; he spends vast sums of money to procure them, and fucks several.

21. This libertine requires a mother and her daughter. He first fucks the mother, then deflowers the daughter while the mother holds her down.

22. This libertine likes adultery only. He requires women who are virtuous and well-behaved by reputation, and ruins them for their husbands.

23. He requires that a husband bring his wife to him as a prostitute, and hold her down while he fucks her.

24. He places a married woman naked on a bed and fucks her while the woman's daughter, suspended above, offers him her cunt to be licked out; then he turns the tables and fucks the daughter while licking clean the mother's arsehole. After tonguing the daughter's cunt, he makes her piss; then he kisses the mother's arsehole and

makes her shit.

25. This libertine has four daughters, legitimate and married. He desires to fuck all four, and makes them all pregnant so that one day he will have the pleasure of deflowering the very children he has conceived by his daughters – children the husbands suppose to be theirs.

26. This libertine has himself wanked while a maid is being fingered about the clitoris. Although he wishes to ejaculate at the same time as the girl, he instead discharges over the buttocks of the man fingering her.

27. This libertine licks the arsehole of one girl while a second girl fingers his arse and a third girl wanks him off; then they exchange tasks so that, when all is done, each of the three has her arse licked out, each wanks the libertine, and each fingers his arsehole. Farts are required of them all.

28. He licks the cunt of one girl while fucking a second in the mouth and while his arsehole is sucked by a third; then the positions are changed. Each cunt must discharge, and he gobbles up the cunt-cream.

29. He sucks a shit-smeared arsehole, has a girl lick clean his own shit-smeared hole, and wanks himself against a third filthy orifice. The three then swap positions.

30. This libertine has two girls wanked by two others before his eyes and alternately fucks the two fricatrices from the rear, in the cunt, while they continue their lesbian caresses.

31. He desires an elder girl to corrupt a younger with bad habits; the elder must wank her, teach her wicked words, and finally hold her down while he fucks her, virgin or not.

32. He summons four women. Two he fucks in the mouth, two in the cunt, taking great care not to insert his cock in a mouth before having first had it up a cunt. While all this is going on, a fifth woman continually reams him with a dildo.

33. This libertine requires a dozen women, six young and six old; if possible, they should be mothers and daughters. He licks out their cunts, arseholes and mouths. When applying his lips to the cunt, he wants copious jets of piss; when at the mouth, torrents of saliva; when at the arse, gusting farts.

34. This libertine employs eight women who wank him; each of the eight must assume a different lewd posture.

35. He wishes to have three men and three women fucking each other in a succession of different positions.

36. He assembles twelve pairs of girls. They are arranged so that only their arses are visible to him, with the rest of their bodies concealed from sight. He wanks himself off while gazing at this buttock sculpture.

37. He has six couples simultaneously wank each other in a room walled with mirrors; each couple is composed of two girls, fingering each other in various, equally lewd postures. He is in the middle of the room and watches both the couples and their multiple reflections. After being

wanked by an old woman, he ejaculates in the midst of it all. He has, of course, kissed the buttocks of every participant in this tableau.

38. This libertine has four whores besot themselves with cheap wine then fight each other while he watches. When they are thoroughly drunk, they one after the other vomit into his mouth. He favours the oldest and ugliest hags possible for this mania.

39. This libertine has a girl shit slowly into his mouth, but does not eat her turd; while she is shitting, a second girl sucks his cock and fingers his arsehole. When he comes, he simultaneously ejaculates and shits into the hand of the girl who is fingering him. The girls then exchange places.

40. He has a man shit into his mouth and eats it while a little boy wanks him with both hands; then the man wanks him while he watches the boy shit.

41. He fucks one girl in the mouth, having just shitted into that very orifice; a second girl is lying atop the first, with the first girl's head between her thighs, and a third girl drops a heavy turd upon the second girl's face. The libertine, while driving his cock into his own turd in the first girl's mouth, eats up the shit deposited by the third girl upon the second's face. Then they alternate roles, so that each girl eventually enacts all three of them.

42. Thirty girls pass through this libertine's hands in one day, and he has each and every one of them shit into his mouth, devouring the turds of the three or four prettiest. He repeats this orgy five times a week, which means he

receives 7,800 girls a year. He is seventy years old and has been in the shit business for fifty.

43. This libertine sees twelve girls every morning and swallows a fresh turd from each, one after the other.

44. He places himself in a bathtub; thirty women come up one after the other and piss and shit into the tub till it's full to the brim. He ejaculates while wallowing in the ordure.

45. He shits in the presence of four women, requiring them not only to watch but to coax out the turds with their fingers. Next, he wishes them to divide up the shit equally and devour it; then each woman shits a turd of her own. He mashes them up and swallows the lot, but his shit-providers must be women of at least sixty years old.

46. He has two girls shit, then forces the second to eat the first's turd, and vice versa. Then both girls shit a further turd, and he devours them both.

47. He assembles a mother and her three daughters, then eats the girls' shit off the mother's buttocks, the mother's shit off the buttocks of the youngest daughter.

48. He obliges a son to shit into his mother's mouth and to then wipe his arse clean with her teats. Next, he eats the turd from the mother's mouth and then has the mother shit into her son's mouth whence, as before, he eats the fresh turd.

49. He makes a father eat his son's shit, then he eats the father's.

50. He has a brother shit into his sister's cunt, and eats up the turd. The sister must then shit into her brother's mouth, whence the libertine also devours this second turd.

51. This libertine wishes a whore, while wanking him, to utter filthy blasphemies; he yells others in return. His amusement during this profane dialogue consists solely of kissing her arse.

52. He wishes a girl to accompany him to a church and wank him off there, especially at the time of holy communion. He sits as near to the altar as possible, and fondles her buttocks while she pumps him.

53. He attends confession with the sole intention of producing an erection in his confessor; to this end he lists the most lubricious sins, wanking himself off in the confession box while he speaks.

54. He bids a girl to make a confession in church, then fucks her in the mouth the minute she emerges.

55. He fucks a whore throughout a Mass being held in his private chapel, and ejaculates furiously at the moment the Host is raised aloft.

56. He bribes a church confessor to yield his place to him, then proceeds to advise the young parishioners who confess to him the most lubricious behaviour while pardoning them all their sins.

57. He bids his daughter go to confess to a monk he has bribed, and secretly watches. The monk demands that the girl keep her skirts raised high over her thighs while

she catalogues her sins, making sure her naked arse is positioned in full view of the father; thus he is able to hear his daughter's confessions while simultaneously contemplating her buttocks.

58. He celebrates a Mass attended by nude whores; while watching this spectacle, he rubs his cock between another girl's buttocks.

59. He bids his wife go and confess to a monk he has bribed; the monk seduces the wife and fucks her while the libertine watches in concealment. Should the wife ever refuse the monk's advances, he springs from hiding and pins her down so the monk may penetrate her.

60. He fucks whores on the holy altar while Mass is proclaimed, their naked arses spread apart on the sacred stone.

61. He has a naked slut sit astride and bend down over a large crucifix, then plunges his cock into her cunt to the hilt; his thrusts make her clitoris grind against Christ's beard.

62. He farts and has a whore fart into the holy chalice, they both piss into it, they both shit into it, and finally he spurts his spunk into the mess.

63. He makes a small boy shit onto the plate of the Eucharist, then devours the turd while the boy suckles his cock.

64. He has two girls shit on a crucifix, then shits on it himself. They then wank him off against the three huge

turds framing Christs's face.

65. He smashes a crucifix and several icons of the Virgin and Eternal Father then shits on the debris and sets fire to the whole lot. Another mania involves bringing a whore to hear the sermon; she wanks him slowly as he listens to the word of God.

66. He takes holy communion then, while the wafer is still in his mouth, has four whores shit upon it.

67. He bids a whore be blessed in holy communion then fucks her in the mouth and arsehole when she returns.

68. He interrupts a priest in the midst of saying Mass in his private chapel, so that a whore can wank him over the chalice; he shoots his spunk into it then has the whore wank the priest until he follows suit. He then forces the priest to drink down the tepid discharges.

69. He intervenes as soon as the Host is consecrated and forces the priest to sodomise a whore with it.

70. He makes a whore fart over the Host, he follows suit, then eats the Host while fucking the whore.

71. He compels a whore to shit on the Host, shits on it himself then hurls it into a privy.

72. He rubs a whore's clitoris with the Host until she drenches it with cunt-cream, then shoves it up her cunt and fucks her, ejaculating over it in turn.

73. He chops the Host up with a dagger, then has a whore ram the pieces up his shit-crusted arsehole.

74. He has himself wanked and discharges furiously over the Host then, once he comes to his senses, feeds it to a pack of dogs.

75. He has himself flogged by one girl during Mass, while another sucks on his cock, and ejaculates when the Host is held aloft.

76. This libertine has two sluts gently whip his arse with a cane; each lays ten stripes, alternately fingering his greased arsehole.

77. He has himself whipped by four different girls while a fifth fires farts down his throat; the girls take turns, so each one both flogs and farts.

78. He makes his wife whip him while he fucks his daughter, next the daughter whips while he fucks his wife; he has first prostituted both bitches in the local whorehouse.

79. He has two girls whip him at once, one striping his front and the other his rear; when he is well and truly aroused, he fucks one of them while the other wields the lash, then vice versa.

80. This libertine has himself horsewhipped while sucking a boy's arsehole and fucking a slut in the mouth; then he fucks the boy's mouth while licking out the girl's arse, all the while being lashed by the second whore. Finally he has the boy whip him while the whore who has

striped him sucks him off and the other one wields the lash.

81. He has himself lashed by an old woman and sucked by an old man, then has their daughter shit into his mouth; roles are exchanged so that, finally, everyone performs each task.

82. He has himself whipped while wanking himself and spunking over a crucifix wedged in a slut's arsehole.

83. He has himself whipped while sodomising a whore, using his cock to drive a Host into her fundament.

84. He is received by an entire brothel; every whore lashes him while his kisses the Madam's arsehole. She farts great gusts of diarrhoea down his gullet.

85. This libertine has himself horsewhipped by teams of buggy drivers and chimney sweeps who pass two at a time, one wielding the lash and the other farting into his mouth; he employs ten or twelve in a single morning.

86. He has himself held down by three girls while a fourth sits astride him and thrashes his haunches; each girl takes her turn to mount and whip him.

87. Naked, he presents himself before six sluts; each knows the role she is to play. Conscience-stricken, he begs to be forgiven for his sins and throws himself prostrate before them. Each slut decrees a penance, and for each he refuses to do he will receive one hundred lashes. The girl he refuses will ply the whip. All the penances are exceedingly depraved: one wishes to shit in his mouth;

another for him to lick her spittle from the floor; a third, who is menstruating heavily, wishes him to swab out her cunt with his tongue; the fourth, who hasn't washed her feet for weeks, bids him lick between her toes; the fifth wishes him to suck the snot from her nose; the last commands him to drink her piss.

88. Fifteen girls arrive in teams of three; one whips his arse, one sucks his cock, the third shits in front of him. Then she who shitted, whips; she who sucked, shits; she who whipped, sucks; and so on until all fifteen girls have performed. He is mindless with ecstasy; a procuress is in charge of proceedings. He repeats this orgy six times a week.

89. Twenty-five nude whores soften up his buttocks with successive slaps and caresses; he is not content until his arse is completely numb.

90. He is put on trial by a jury of six whores; each knows the role she is to play. They sentence him to be hanged and he is indeed strung up; but the rope snaps at the last minute, just as his erect cock discharges.

91. He arranges six old, drooling women in a semi-circle; while three sluts with shaved cunts lash him, the six crones spit in his face.

92. One girl reams this libertine's arsehole with the butt of a cat o'nine tails while another whips his thighs and cock from the front; he thus eventually sprays his spunk over the bare tits of the slut before him.

93. Two whores flay him with a bullwhip while a third,

kneeling before him, wanks him with both fists until he jets hot spunk over her naked tits.

94. Stripped naked, he struggles against six women, pretending to avoid the cut of their whips; he tries to snatch the whips from their hands, but they overwhelm him.

95. He runs the gauntlet between two files of twelve young girls apiece, all wielding whips. They whip his nude body from head to foot, and he ejaculates during the ninth race.

96. He has the soles of his feet whipped, followed by his cock, then his thighs while, as he lies on a couch, three pregnant women successively sit astride him and shit in his mouth.

97. Three girls alternately thrash him; one with a cane, the other with a bullwhip, the third with a cat o'nine tails. A fourth, kneeling before the libertine as his henchman fingers her greased arsehole, sucks upon his prick while whipping the henchman's, which finally shoots hot spunk over the girl's buttocks.

98. Six girls surround the libertine. One pricks him with a needle, the second tears his flesh with pincers, the third burns him, the fourth bites him, the fifth scratches his skin away, the sixth whips him. This is done all over his body, and he ejaculates like a horse in the midst of it.

99. This libertine has himself wanked by his henchman while a nude whore balances on a narrow beam; whilst he is being wanked, she may not move an inch or topple off.

100. He has a procuress wank him off while he fingers the crack between her buttocks; meanwhile, a whore must hold a lighted candle which she may not drop until the libertine has discharged every drop of his spunk. He is careful not to ejaculate until the hot wax has seared her fingers.

101. He dines at an immense table. For light, he has six blazing candles whose ends have been screwed into the arseholes of six nude whores crouching on the tabletop.

102. While he dines, he has a whore squat naked on sharp pebbles; if she stirs but once during his meal, she is packed off home and not paid a sou. Above her are two lighted candles whose molten wax drips constantly onto her back and breasts.

103. He confines a slut in a narrow iron cage for four days, so that she can neither sit nor lie down; he feeds her through the bars like a she-beast.

104. This libertine wraps up a girl and a cat in a blanket and makes the girl prance about; the cat bites and scratches her as she falls to the floor. He compels her to get up again and to continue her agonizing dance until he ejaculates.

105. He massages a woman from head to foot with a substance which causes her skin to itch so violently that she scratches herself till her she is raw and bloody; he watches her frenzy, wanking all the while.

106. He gives a woman a potion to drink which dams up her womb so she cannot menstruate and her body is

poisoned.

107. He makes one woman drink horse medicine; she collapses with hideous stomach cramps and he gloats all day as she vomits and shits.

108. He rubs a nude girl's nipples and cunt-lips with honey, then ties her to a column and releases a swarm of hungry flies upon her.

109. He straps a girl on a wheel which spins at prodigious speed. She is naked and spins until he shoots his spunk over her.

110. He hangs another girl by her heels until his spunk is loosed.

111. He feeds a whore a heavy dose of emetic, tells her she is poisoned, then wanks furiously at the sight of her puking and shitting.

112. This libertine kneads and squeezes a whore until her tits are completely black and blue.

113. He kneads and batters her arse for three hours flat, and repeats this abuse for nine days in a row.

114. This libertine makes a girl climb a tall ladder until she is twenty feet in the air, and which point a rung breaks and she plummets onto mattresses prepared in advance. He approaches and sprays hot spunk in her face, or sometimes in her cunt, the moment she lands.

115. He slaps a slut's face as hard as he can and sprays

it with spunk while doing so. He is seated in an armchair, she kneels naked before him.

116. He beats her knuckles bloody with a wooden ruler.

117. He slaps her across the arse until her buttocks bleed.

118. He inserts the nozzle of a bellows in her arsehole and pumps air into her bowels.

119. He gives her an enema of near-boiling water then wanks like a devil as she writhes and shits in agony, finally ejaculating over her buttocks.

120. This libertine kidnaps some nuns, beats them with a crucifix and rosaries, then has each pose as a statue of the Virgin upon the altar. They are not permitted to move from this cramped position for the duration of a lengthy Mass; when at last the Host is raised aloft, they must shit loudly in unison upon the altar-top.

121. This libertine has a serving-wench run naked around a midnight garden in the freezing dead of winter; here and there are stretched cords over which she trips and falls.

122. He strips her naked and casts her, as if by accident, into a vat of near-boiling water. She may not climb out until he has first spurted his spunk over her body.

123. He ties her naked to a pole in a garden on a winter's day. She must remain there until she has completed five Hail Marys and five Pater Nosters, or until

another girl who is wanking him off has managed to make his spunk fly as he contemplates the spectacle.

124. He spreads a powerful glue around the rim of a metal privy then sends a girl in to shit; when she sits, her arse is caught fast. Meanwhile, he introduces a small charcoal brazier and heats the seat beneath her buttocks. Scorched, she leaps up, leaving an almost perfect circle of bloody skin behind her.

125. He gets a girl thoroughly drunk, so that she passes out. While asleep, her bed is raised. In the middle of the night, she gropes for her chamber pot; not finding it, she reaches further and plunges out of bed onto another mattress below. The libertine, lying in wait, springs on top of her and rapes her as she gibbers like a wine-sot.

126. He has one whore run naked around the garden and chases her brandishing a horsewhip, but only threatens her with it. She nonetheless runs until she collapses with exhaustion, at which point he falls upon her and drives his cock into her sweaty arsehole.

127. This libertine likes to lash girls with one hundred strokes, ten at a time, using a switch of black silk. Between each set of blows he deliriously kisses and licks her arsehole.

128. He whips one girl with a cat o'nine tails whose thongs have been steeped in vintage brandy, and does not shed his spunk until her blood is flowing in torrents; he sprays it into the weals on her buttocks.

129. This libertine will only whip girls between the ages

of five and seven, and always finds some pretext so it seems he is punishing them for a misdemeanour.

130. This libertine poses as a priest and takes confession from a woman. She recites all her sins; far from pardoning her, he gives her five hundred frenzied lashes of the bullwhip.

131. He clamps four women in chains and gives each six hundred lashes.

132. He has the ceremony repeated in his presence by two henchmen, one relieving the other when his arm is fatigued by the whipping. Twenty women are dealt with, each receiving six hundred strokes; they are not bound but chased round the chamber like cattle. He wanks himself as the mayhem proceeds.

133. This libertine will only whip boys aged from fourteen to sixteen, and requires them to ejaculate into his mouth afterward. Each boy takes one hundred lashes, and he deals with two at each sitting.

134. This libertine has a naked slut enter a chamber, whereupon two of his henchmen leap out, tie her up and whip her buttocks, one apiece, until the skin is flayed off. Afterwards he wanks the two men by rubbing their cocks against her bleeding arse, then sprays his own seed over the wounds.

135. He binds one slut hand and foot to a dungeon wall. Facing her, and also attached to the wall, is a razor-sharp steel blade adjusted to the height of her belly. He then proceeds to whip her ferociously. If she strives to avoid his

blows, the blade slices her belly open; if she recoils from the blade, his whipstrokes lay her spine bare.

136. One girl he thrashes for nine days, giving her one hundred strokes on the first day, two hundred on the second, three hundred on the third, and so on until she dies.

137. He forces a naked whore down on all fours then climbs on her back, facing her buttocks, with his legs clamped tight about her ribcage. Once in the saddle, he brings his cat o'nine tails down upon her arse-cheeks with such venom that the thongs curl round to her cunt. In this way he ensures that the steel tips shoot right up her, tearing out chunks of vaginal flesh with every blow.

138. For this mania he must have a pregnant woman. He ties her bent backwards over a large cylinder, her head secured to the seat of a chair and her legs spread as far apart as possible. Her swollen belly is stretched to the limit, her cunt yawns in his face. He then thrashes her belly with a horsewhip until blood pours out; at which point he walks round to the other side of the cylinder and wanks into her face.

139. This libertine only employs girls of fifteen, whipping them with switches of stinging nettles and holly until their buttocks bleed. His taste in arses is highly sophisticated, he is not easy to please.

140. This libertine likes to thrash women with a barbed bullwhip, and will not cease until their arses are in tatters. He uses four women, one after the other.

141. This libertine will only beat his slaves with steel-tipped canes, and discharges only when they are drowned in rivers of blood.

142. This libertine also requires pregnant women; he carves chunks of flesh from their buttocks with a bullwhip, occasionally delivering a swipe to their heavy bellies.

143. This libertine places a candle on a high shelf. He then attaches to the middle finger of a whore's right hand a piece of bread soaked in tallow and set afire; to avoid being burnt, she must light the candle with it. She must leap high in the air to reach the shelf, and the libertine, armed with a leather-thonged whip, lashes her with all his might to encourage her. If she succeeds, the game is done; if she fails, she is scorched and then whipped until she falls unconscious.

144. This libertine thrashes first his wife, then his daughter, then hauls them bleeding to the local brothel to sell them into prostitution.

145. This libertine likes to string up a nude slut then set about her with a barbed cat o'nine tails, lashing her from the nape of her neck to the calves of her legs. He is only sated when the entire skin of her back and buttocks has been removed.

146. This libertine will only whip breasts, and exceedingly large ones at that. He always pays double if the whore is pregnant.

147. This libertine will only whip the face, and uses a switch of dried twigs; the faces must be extremely pretty.

148. Using switches, this libertine lashes the entire body, face, cunt, and tits included.

149. This libertine gives two hundred blows of the bullwhip, these being evenly distributed up and down the backs of lads aged between sixteen and twenty.

150. This libertine waits in a room; four girls set about him and soundly whip him. When he is fully aroused he falls upon a fifth girl, who is naked and awaits him in the adjoining chamber. Armed with a bullwhip he lashes every part of her he can, maintaining a torrent of blows until he ejaculates. When merciful – which is seldom – he shuns the second room till his discharge is nigh, thus sparing the fifth girl's agonies.

TWO

The Circle Of Blood

1. This libertine loves nothing but to have himself buggered; he scours the land high and low for youths with huge, thick, sweaty cocks.

2. This libertine will only deflower little girls between the ages of three and seven, and then only anally. He is enormously rich, and has a cock of colossal size; his discharge lasts six minutes, and he bellows like a bull while it is in progress.

3. This libertine sodomises boys exclusively, and only on the exact stroke of their seventh birthday.

4. This libertine entertains a boy of fifteen and his thirteen-year-old sister. He urges the boy to fuck her, and while they are in each other's clutches he sodomises them in turn.

5. He has himself buggered while buggering a boy and then the boy's sister.

6. He has four girls fart in his mouth whilst he buggers a fifth, then changes girls in rotation; all fart, all are buggered, and he does not ejaculate until the fifth arsehole

is well and truly reamed.

7. He buggers three lads and has each of them shit, wanking the one whose arse is stoppered.

8. He fucks a girl in the mouth while her brother shits into his mouth, then reverses their roles; during each operation he has himself buggered by a henchman with a huge cock.

9. This libertine will only bugger girls of fifteen, and only after whipping them till the skin hangs off their buttocks.

10. This libertine trusses up a nude slut, pinches and tweaks her buttocks and arsehole for an hour, then buggers her while his henchman thrashes her with extreme violence.

11. This libertine will only commit sodomy during holy Mass; he shoots his spunk up a youth's arse the minute the Host is raised aloft.

12. This libertine buggers a prostitute while kicking a crucifix around in the dirt; he encourages her to piss on it.

13. He has a whore shit copiously and smears most of it around her arsehole. He then tamps a consecrated Host into the opening with his enormous cock.

14. He buggers one youth while a second buggers him, both driving a consecrated Host into the arse of their catamite. Another Host rests on the neck of the youth he is buggering, and a third youth is called to shit upon it. As

the shit drops he shoots his seed, screaming dreadful blasphemies.

15. He buggers a priest in the midst of saying Mass, withdrawing only when the priest has finished his consecration; the priest quickly shoves the Host up his arse, and the libertine rams his cock in again, driving the holy wafer into the clergyman's bowels.

16. This libertine only sodomises very ancient women, and only while they are being soundly horsewhipped.

17. This libertine only sodomises elderly men, and only while himself being buggered by a well-endowed youth.

18. This libertine regularly sodomises his own son.

19. This libertine will only sodomise negroes, hunchbacks or cripples.

20. Seeking to combine incest, adultery, sodomy and blasphemy, this libertine buggers his newly-wed daughter with a Host.

21. This libertine has two henchmen alternately fuck and flagellate him while he buggers a young boy and while an old man shits into his mouth. He devours the turd.

22. Two lackeys take turns fucking him, one in the mouth, the other up the arse. This carries on for no less than three hours. He swallows the spunk of the mouth-fucker with alacrity.

23. He has himself sodomised by a gang of ten men,

whom he pays by the discharge; in the space of a morning he pays out as many as twenty-four times.

24. He prostitutes his wife, sister, and daughter, and watches gleefully as they are sodomised by scoundrels.

25. He employs eight men; one fucks him in the mouth, one up his arse, one beneath his left testicle, one beneath his right; he wanks two others, one in each hand; a seventh is lodged between his thighs and the eighth must wank in his face.

26. This libertine has an elderly man buggered before him by one of his henchmen. Several times during the proceedings the henchman withdraws his cock and places it to the lips of his master, who sucks it clean. The libertine then sucks the dotard's cock, licks out his shit-clogged arsehole, then drives his own cock deep inside it while the henchman now buggers his master, his lusty pelvic thrusts spurred by the lashstrokes of the libertine's governess (for he is but a young man).

27. While viciously buggering a fifteen-year-old girl, he strangles and chokes her so her ringpiece contracts; all the while he has himself bullwhipped.

28. He has large globules of quicksilver shoved into his bowels. These spheres rise up and down, giving him excessive pleasure, and in a delirium he sucks cocks, swallows hot spunk, and eats great lumps of shit from whores' unwashed arses. His ecstasy lasts for over two hours.

29. This libertine would be buggered by a father while

he in turn buggers that father's son and daughter.

30. This libertine fucks a turkey whose head is gripped between the thighs of a nude, prostrate girl, so it appears he is buggering her. As he pumps away his valet sodomises him without mercy, and at the moment he ejaculates, the girl slits the turkey's throat.

31. He fucks a she-goat from behind while being soundly whipped. The goat conceives and gives birth to a monster; monster though it be, he buggers it.

32. He buggers male deer in the forest.

33. He wishes to see a woman orgasm as a dog licks out her cunt; the very moment she comes, he blows the dog's head off with a pistol. The woman is unharmed.

34. He buggers a swan after coining a Host up its anus, and throttles it to death as he discharges.

35. This libertine is placed naked in a large whicker structure with a hole at one end, and presses his gaping arsehole to the opening after greasing it with the cunt-cream of a brood mare. The structure is shaped like a horse, and is covered with a horsehair skin. A stallion is fetched in and straightway mounts the artificial mare, embedding its three-foot cock into his arse while he in turn buggers the pretty white bitch-dog he has with him in the basket.

36. In a similar basket he constrains a woman, who is duly sodomised by a bull with a huge, tufted pizzle. He watches her sufferings with glee.

37. He has a pet snake which he is fond of squeezing headfirst up his anus; while being thus sodomised, he furiously buggers a cat which is tied in a basket so its claws may not tatter his testicles.

38. Using an elaborate machine, he fucks a she-donkey while himself being buggered by a mule with a seven-foot pizzle.

39. He fucks the nostrils of a goat which is all the while licking his balls; during this folly, he is alternately whipped and has his arsehole licked out.

40. He buggers a ram while a dog licks the shit from his arsehole.

41. He buggers a dog whose head is cut off with a sword the moment he ejaculates.

42. He pays a whore to wank a monkey, and is buggered as he observes this amusing spectacle.

43. He fucks a monkey's arsehole; the monkey is strapped in a basket and is tormented by lackeys as the libertine buggers it, so its anus will constrict about his cock.

44. This libertine orders a procuress to fetch him girls guilty of some crime. He arrives and frightens them, saying they will surely be arrested; in the end he offers them protection on condition they allow him to give a good whipping. They agree, and he whips them till they bleed.

45. He has a woman with beautiful hair brought to him,

saying he wishes only to examine her tresses. He then hacks it off with rusty scissors, and discharges his spunk like a madman upon seeing her tears and hearing her wails of misery.

46. He has a young girl enter a dark room, where she can see no-one but hears a conversation regarding her. The conversation is of a nature designed to scare her witless. Suddenly, she receives a deluge of slaps and blows from unseen assailants; she hears the bellows of the libertine as he discharges, then she is slung out on her ear.

47. He has another maid enter a subterranean tomb, lit only by a few dim lamps. After a few moments, during which she sees how hideous a place it is, the lamps are extinguished and a cacophony of screams and rattling chains assails her ears. She faints dead away and at once the libertine falls upon her and buggers her. Spent, he abandons her, and valets come to her rescue; only the youngest, most inexperienced girls are suitable for this scenario.

48. Another girl is lured to the crypt. She is attacked in the dark, stripped naked, and hurled into a coffin. The coffin lid is nailed shut, and the libertine spurts his spunk in time with the rhythm of the hammers.

49. This libertine desires the corpse of a beautiful, recently murdered girl to be placed naked on a bed covered in black satin sheets. He fondles the body, licks out every crevice, and finally buggers it.

50. He next desires two corpses, one of a boy and one of a girl. He buggers the youth's dead body while kissing

the cold white buttocks of the girl's and driving his tongue into the dank anus.

51. This libertine entertains a young whore in a room filled with extremely realistic wax dummies of corpses. Each is pierced and wounded by daggers in various ways; he announces his intention of killing the girl, and lets her select the wound of her choice.

52. He takes her to the next chamber and binds her tight to a real corpse, knee to knee, mouth to mouth, and whips her till the back of her body spurts rivers of blood.

53. This libertine requires a menstruating girl. She arrives at his home and a valet shows her to a cellar room where the libertine awaits her. He is standing next to a pool of icy water, twelve feet across and eight deep, which is concealed from the girl's view. As she approaches him he pushes her into it, discharging into his breeks the minute he hears the splash. She is saved from drowning, but suffers severe illness as a result of the ordeal.

54. He lowers a naked whore into a very deep well and shouts to her that he is about to fill it with large rocks. He flings in a few clods of earth to frighten her then wanks himself off into the well, his spunk landing on the screaming slut's head.

55. This libertine has a pregnant whore brought before him. He terrifies her with insults and threats then severely horsewhips her, continuing this abuse until she either miscarries on the spot, or does so when she returns home. Should she disgorge the foetus while under his roof, he pays her double.

56. This libertine locks a girl into a pitch-black dungeon filled with cats, rats and mice, and tells her she is to be incarcerated there for life. Every day he goes up to the door and banters with her whilst wanking himself off.

57. This libertine bends a nude slut over his knee, sticks bundles of straw in her arsehole, then sets fire to them and watches her buttocks sizzle as the straws burn short.

58. This libertine ties a girl to a St Andrew's cross suspended in the air then whips her with all his might, flaying all the skin from her back. After this, he cuts her down and hurls her headfirst through a first storey-window; mattresses are there to break her fall, and he spurts his seed as he hears her land.

59. He makes one whore swallow a hallucinogenic drug, then kisses her arse as she begins to see terrible things in the room. She imagines the room is being flooded, sees the water rise, and climbs up on a chair; but the water seems to surge higher and the libertine urges her to dive in and swim for it; she plunges, but falls straight onto the stone floor, and he ejaculates at the noise of her bones breaking.

60. Another girl he has suspended by a rope that runs up through a pulley affixed to the top of a tower; he stands at the tower window, she hangs outside and directly opposite him. First he makes her shit in mid-air, then has himself whipped to the bone and wanks himself like a demon, threatening to slice through the rope as he spurts great clots of hot spunk over her tits.

61. He strings up a slut on four thin cords, each attached to one of her limbs. She is held there in agony while a trap door beneath her is opened to reveal a blazing charcoal brazier; should the cords break, she will plunge onto it. The libertine plucks the cords, strains them, and finally cuts one at the moment he discharges. Another time he strings a girl up, places a weight upon her belly, then suddenly jerks all four strings up, rupturing her stomach and tearing her muscles. She must hang there in agony until he shoots his spunk.

62. He binds a whore to a foot stool. A dagger with a needle-sharp point is suspended above her head, hanging by a hair; if the hair snaps, the blade will drive into her skull and brain. The libertine wanks himself in a frenzy as he gloats over his victim's anxious contortions. After an hour of torture, he frees her and proceeds to bloody her buttocks with the same dagger, jabbing her till she admits it pricks most handsomely, then finally sprays her blood-soaked arse with spunk.

63. This libertine violently buggers a young nun who knows nothing of the world, splitting her arse open, and as he spurts his spunk deep into her bowels he fires off two pistol shots next to her ear. The gun-powder sets her hair on fire.

64. This libertine bids his victim sit in an armchair balanced on springs. Her weight releases a number of springs connected to iron rings, which crush her ribcage against the chair. Then by levers and gears he advances twenty daggers until their points pierce her skin; he wanks himself whilst explaining that the least movement of the chair will cause the daggers to stab forward fatally. Finally

he sprays hot spunk into her eyes and nostrils, and as he does so touches the chair, ever so slightly, with his toe.

65. He casts a whore into a crypt hung with deaths-heads and black shrouds, where she sees wax dummies of ghosts about to penetrate every orifice of her body with swords, lances, daggers, spikes and needles. Overcome by fright, she faints; the libertine rushes out to catch her, strips and catwhips her till she revives, then buggers her and discharges heartily into her entrails.

66. A whore is sent into a room in a tower, with a large brazier at its centre. Upon a table are a dagger and a phial of poison; the libertine allows her to choose the means of her death. In most cases she chooses the poison, which is in fact an opiate which sends her into a deep sleep; while she is unconscious, he buggers her furiously, yelling blasphemies and spitting into the brazier.

67. This libertine performs an elaborate ceremony in which he buggers a young girl on a chopping-block, then pretends to decapitate her. Just as the axe falls, a rope snatches her back and the blade buries in the wood. If the rope is not pulled fast enough, her head is forfeit. He soaks his breeks in spunk as the axe falls.

68. He puts a noose around a whore's neck and strings her up with her feet on a stool to which another rope is tied. He sits in an armchair, watching while the whore's daughter suckles his cock. As he discharges he yanks the rope; the whore hangs. He leaves and his lackeys cut the whore down, then revive her with leeches. Meanwhile the libertine beds the daughter, sodomising her brutally all night long while crowing that he has killed her mother.

69. This libertine likes to drag a girl around the room by her ears, discharging as he goes.

70. This libertine gets a nude slut and pinches her everywhere except the tits, until she turns black and blue.

71. He next pinches her tits, punches them, mangles them with pliers until they too are bruised and bloody.

72. He then writes obscene words and signs around her nipples, working with a quill whose tip is steeped in poison; her tits become gangrenous and she suffers the agonies of the damned.

73. He drives over one thousand barbed needles into the infected tits, and sprays them with spunk when every pore is pierced.

74. This libertine buries huge hatpins into every inch of a whore's body, and discharges as the last pin plunges into her nipple.

75. This libertine gives a woman copious amounts to eat and drink, then sews up her cunt and arsehole. He watches in delight as she cries and near faints with the need to shit and piss, finally discharging his seed as the stitches burst.

76. This libertine places a girl in a room. Four henchmen enter and cuff, strike and kick her till she falls down. All four wank each other and spray their spunk over her prostrate, bleeding body.

77. He lodges another girl within an airtight helmet. She

is deprived of oxygen, then given some, then deprived again until her face turns blue.

78. This libertine straps a naked slut belly-down on his dining-table then eats a piping hot omelette off her arse-cheeks. He uses an exceedingly sharp fork.

79. This libertine immobilises a whore's head above a grill, ignites the fire, and buggers her slowly and surely as she roasts.

80. He gently toasts the skin of her tits and buttocks, proceeding inch by inch, using sulphur-tipped matches.

81. He lights candles then extinguishes them again and again by snuffing them out in her cunt, in her arsehole, and against her nipples.

82. He sears her eyelids with a sulphur match; she can no longer sleep, for her eyes will not close.

83. He points a pistol at a prostitute's heart and forces her to chew and swallow a live coal; he then washes out her cunt with a douche of sulphuric acid.

84. This libertine has naked a whore dance around four pillars; the path she must take is strewn with broken glass, shards of metal and nails. A man stands by each pillar, and lashes part of her body every time she passes. The number of times each whore must run this gauntlet depends upon her beauty; the more attractive she is, the more she is thrashed.

85. This libertine punches a whore in the face until her

nose bleeds; he carries on until he discharges, and his spunk mingles with her blood.

86. He pinches and sears her flesh with red-hot pincers, especially her buttocks, breasts and pubic mound.

87. He makes her recline naked and places little piles of gunpowder on her, particularly around her cunt and nipples, then sets fire to them.

88. He licks her arsehole then funnels gunpowder into her cunt; he ignites the powder and ejaculates upon seeing flames blast out of her labia.

89. He soaks her from head to foot with brandy, then puts a match to her. He wanks furiously at the sight of the flambé'd whore, repeating the operation three or four times before shooting his spunk onto her charred belly.

90. He gives her an enema of boiling oil.

91. He whips her cunt until it bleeds, then plunges a red-hot poker into it and another up her arsehole.

92. This libertine likes to trample on a pregnant woman until she aborts; he then thrashes the foetus to shreds with a bullwhip.

93. This libertine has a pretty young girl wank him off, and all the while he caresses her tenderly. At the moment he discharges, he grabs her violently by the hair and drives her head into the wall, dashing her brains out.

94. The previous four libertines assemble once a month

and convene a court. A girl is tried and judged, and each sentences her individually. She receives one hundred strokes of the lash, each libertine meting out twenty-five; the first stripes her from the back to the loins, the second from the loins to the calves, the third from the neck to the navel, including her breasts, and the fourth from the belly to the shins.

95. With a hatpin, this libertine stabs a slut in both eyes, pierces each nipple, and finally impales her clitoris.

96. He pours molten wax over her breasts, into her cunt, and then seals up her anus.

97. He opens up the veins in her left arm and bleeds her like a pig until she expires.

98. This libertine makes a whore strip nude and shit on the floor. Then he cuts open both wrists and makes her stand up while he bleeds her; now and again he whips her for good measure. This continues for an hour, and he only ejaculates when she finally collapses.

99. He cuts one bitch open at the wrists, heels and jugular, and wanks himself into a frenzy watching the five fountains of spurting blood.

100. He scarifies a whore with a carving-knife, concentrating on her buttocks but sparing her tits.

101. Another he scarifies more vigorously, cutting deep into her tits and nipples, and then ringing her arsehole with gashes. He next cauterizes the wounds with a red-hot iron.

102. This libertine has himself bound hand and foot like a beast and then draped in a tiger skin. A plump, nude whore is placed opposite him, tied by her neck to the ceiling and by her feet to the floor so she cannot move. Then the libertine has himself wanked, whipped, poked, fingered round the arsehole, and generally roused to a frenzy; his henchmen release him and he leaps upon the girl with a roar. He bites her all over, especially her clitoris and nipples, which he chews off. He shrieks and bellows like a rabid beast, and discharges great gouts of spunk over the floor. Finally the girl shits in fear, and he devours her turds gluttonously.

103. This libertine has a nude slut spreadeagled before him. He pulls her back teeth out with pliers then lacerates her bloody gums with red-hot needles.

104. He breaks her fingers with the pliers, one by one.

105. Using a heavy hammer, he mashes one of her feet to pulp.

106. He cuts off one of her hands, slowly sawing through the wrist.

107. While shooting his spunk over her, he knocks her front teeth out with a hammer; he has the greatest pleasure in sucking her bloody mouth before proceeding to the next stage of his mania.

108. He amputates her good foot with a rusty saw.

109. He smashes one of her arms with a crowbar while buggering her.

110. He shatters her shinbone then buggers her again.

111. He ties her to a stepladder, then fixes a rope to the rungs; he pulls the rope at random so that the ladder falls. The first time she breaks one limb, the next another.

112. He cuts off one of her ears.

113. He slits her lips and nostrils.

114. He sucks and bites her tongue, then pierces it with a sharp hot iron.

115. He rips several fingernails out, followed by most of her toenails.

116. He severs one of her fingers at the base joint and stuffs it up her arse.

117. He fires fifteen or twenty drops of molten lead into her mouth then burns her gums with acid.

118. This libertine makes a whore lick clean his shit-clogged arsehole then snips off the end of her tongue with scissors; having thus mutilated her, he buggers her without mercy.

119. This libertine uses a machine which drills through bodies with a hollow steel bit, extracting cylindrical gobbets of flesh when removed; if not withdrawn, the machine bores on automatically.

120. He takes a boy of ten or twelve and castrates him.

121. He raises and isolates each nipple with a pair of pliers, then snips off each one with scissors.

122. This libertine sucks a whore's mouth and tongue with great vigour then smashes a glass bottle against her face.

123. He tears off both her legs, ties one arm behind her back, places a little stick in her free hand and tells her to defend herself. Then he sets about her with a cavalry sword, cutting and wounding her with great dexterity; finally shooting his spunk into her gaping body as she expires.

124. Another girl is crucified and the libertine breaks her limbs with a hammer.

125. Pistol in hand, this libertine has a fat whore stand sideways to him then lets off a shot which grazes both breasts. His aim is to shoot off her nipples.

126. He makes her crouch down twenty feet away and present her buttocks to him; he fires a bullet straight up her gaping arsehole.

127. This libertine horsewhips a pregnant woman across the belly until she miscarries; he then makes her eat the raw foetus.

128. He whips a lad of sixteen or seventeen, thoroughly buggers him and then neatly shears off his genitals and feeds them to his hounds.

129. This libertine demands a virgin be brought before

him; he slices off her clitoris with a razor then deflowers her with a heated steel dildo, driving it home with two-fisted hammer blows.

130. This libertine desires only women eight months pregnant; he performs abortions on them by forcing them to drink a poison which flushes out the child. His other skill is to induce birth through the arsehole, ripping out the dead foetus in a shower of blood and shit.

131. This libertine is a torturer; he has a gallery of wretched sluts tied nude in a dungeon. He severs one's arm.

132. He cuts off another's hands at the wrists and seals the stumps with a hot iron.

133. He cuts out her tongue by the roots and cauterizes her mouth with a hot iron.

134. He has a hooded henchman amputate one of her legs while he buggers her.

135. He pulls out all her teeth with pliers and replaces each one with a red-hot nail, which he secures in place by hammer-blows; he does this straight after fucking the whore in the mouth.

136. He gouges out one eye.

137. He drips molten wax into another's eyes, blinding her and finally dissolving both eyeballs.

138. He lops off her nipple, cooks it on a griddle and

eats it; then neatly slices off the whole breast, cauterizing the wound with a hot brand.

139. He buggers a slut, decimating her arsehole, then horsewhips her buttocks to shreds; what meat remains he pares off with a razor, cooks and eats with a fine red wine.

140. He lops off both her ears with secateurs.

141. He cuts off all her extremities: ten fingers, ten toes, two nipples, one clitoris and the end of her tongue.

142. He carves away several chunks of flesh from various parts of one whore's body, then has them roasted and obliges her to dine with him.

143. He amputates all four limbs from a young lad then sodomises the torso. He seals the wounds, feeds the lad and thus keeps him alive for nearly a year, buggering him ruthlessly day and night.

144. He chains one of the girl's hands to the wall, then leaves her to starve. Just beyond reach he places an excellent meal, and next to her a large knife. To eat, she must carve through her own forearm; otherwise, she dies of starvation. He watches her plight through a window, wanking himself and laughing like the devil.

145. He manacles a mother and daughter; to survive, one of them must reach the food placed just out of reach, which means sacrificing a hand. He delights in listening to them discuss their dilemma.

146. He plucks out both a whore's eyes and leaves her

locked in a room barefoot, telling her that food is there but she must get up and search for it. To reach the food she must traverse a plate of red-hot iron, which of course she cannot see. He amuses himself observing her plight; will she risk burning the skin from her feet, or starve?

147. He submits a whore to rope torture, binding all four limbs to ropes, raising her high in the air, then letting her drop suddenly. The ropes violently break her fall a foot above the ground. This is repeated, and each time a limb is dislocated or broken.

148. He lacerates her entire body with deep knife-wounds then pours boiling pitch and lead into them.

149. The moment a pregnant woman gives birth, he binds her hand and foot and ropes the infant across the room from her. She is unable to reach the wailing brat, and must watch it expire. Once it dies he steps up and applies fearsome whipstrokes to her cunt, making sure the steel tips of the tongs penetrate and lacerate her. He himself is usually the child's father.

<u>THREE</u>

The Circle Of Manias

1. This libertine likes to sodomise beggarwomen who've starved for several days. He also likes to lock them up in his dungeon until they die of hunger; he watches closely as they suffer, wanking himself noon till night, but never discharges until the day they perish.

2. He keeps one hag in a prison cell, gradually reducing the amount of food she is given over a period of months. Each night she shits, each night he devours the diminishing turds.

3. In his youth he liked to suck a maiden's mouth and drink her saliva; now, his passion is to lock a girl up in a dungeon with food for only twenty days. On the thirtieth day he wanks over the corpse.

4. First, this libertine has a girl piss into his mouth; then he slowly destroys her by preventing her from drinking ever again, though he feeds her all the while.

5. This libertine whips a woman to shreds, then kills her through sleep deprivation.

6. This libertine used to love making a whore shit, so

he might devour the turds even as they emerged, hot and steaming, from her arsehole. Now he feeds her only on stale bread and cheap wine, and she soon dies of malnutrition.

7. In his youth, this libertine was a renowned cunt-fucker; now he injects women with venereal diseases so virulent that they die in agony after a very short time.

8. He also adored drinking whores' vomit straight from their lips; now, he pours in a poisonous concoction which causes them swift and ghastly death from fever.

9. His greatest delight used to be digging shit from a slut's arsehole with his fingers; now, he administers enemas of boiling oil or sulphuric acid.

10. This libertine used to a whipsman of great repute; now, he binds his victims to a pivot upon which they revolve until death intercedes.

11. He used to revel in merely slapping a whore's face; now, as a mature man, he prefers to twist her head right around until it stares backwards. In this way, he may simultaneously gloat over her tortured face and her buttocks.

12. Addicted to bestiality as a youngster, as an adult this libertine prefers to see a virgin's cunt split open by a snorting stallion; the girl invariably dies.

13. Once the greatest sodomist alive, this libertine now buries little girls up to the waist in quicklime, and keeps them there till their lower halves rot.

14. In youth, he was fond of stroking a girl's clitoris; now he has girls held down and scours their cunts with steel wool until they pass out or expire.

15. Gradually perfecting his art on various parts of the body over the years, this famous whip-wielder now thrashes a bitch from head to toe until she's flayed alive; he wears her skin to dinner.

16. This libertine used to squeeze a girl's throat during sodomy, to tighten her anus; now he ties her by a noose. A meal is placed before her, but to reach it she must strangle. Otherwise, she starves to death.

17. This libertine used to adore fondling a whore's tits and buttocks; now he lambastes them with such abominable fury that his victim soon expires in a welter of blood.

18. This libertine used to like slowly bleeding his women; now he opens up their arteries so savagely that they die within minutes.

19. In youth, this libertine would whip a naked whore around a room till she dropped from exhaustion; now, he wraps her in blankets and shuts her in a steaming bath-house where she suffocates to death.

20. Once upon a time, he liked to be attired in nappies and fed whoreshit with a silver spoon; now he wraps a bitch so tightly in swaddling clothes that he crushes her lungs.

21. This libertine once had a great passion for bestiality;

now, he likes to sew up a girl inside an untanned donkey's skin, with only her head protruding. He feeds and cares for her until the animal's hide shrinks and shoots her entrails out of her mouth.

22. Where once he hung a girl upside-down for fun, he now swings her up on a meathook till her brain drowns in blood.

23. This libertine, who used to make his sluts drunk, now funnels wine into their bellies till they explode.

24. This libertine used to tweak nipples; now he buckles an iron pot over each of his slut's breasts and lowers her onto a hot stove; the pots heat up and burn her till she dies in agony.

25. As a lad, this libertine used to watch women swim naked. Now, he throws a whore headfirst into a pond, drags her out half-drowned, and hangs her by her heels to drain her off. Once she comes to he hurls her back in, drags her out again, and so on until she expires.

26. This libertine used to enjoy kicking a slut's arse so she stumbled against a brazier. Now he makes a nun stand upright between two blazing fires; one cooks her in front, one from behind, and there she must remain till the fat on her body melts.

27. This libertine used to restrict a woman's breathing by choking or masking the nose and mouth. Now, he shoves a naked whore beneath four mattresses; he and his henchmen bounce on top till she suffocates.

28. He used to offer his victims three ways of dying; now, he simply buggers them and, upon discharging, blows their brains out with a shotgun.

29. This libertine was fond of wrapping a girl up in a blanket with a cat; now, he hurls her naked from the top of his tower onto sharp gravel fifty feet below. He spurts his spunk after her upon hearing her land.

30. This libertine was ever fond of constricting a whore's throat as he buggered her. Now he slips a black silk cord about her neck and throttles her to death during his orgasm.

31. He once liked to fuck drugged prostitutes; now he kills them with an overdose of opium and buggers them in their death coma.

32. This libertine used to give women duckings; now he ties heavy stones about their necks and lets them drown.

33. Once, this libertine was content to slap a whore's face; now, he pours molten lead into her ears while she sleeps.

34. Other girls, whom he once would have whipped, he dispatches with a mighty hammer blow to the skull.

35. Where once this libertine would let a candle burn out in a whore's arsehole, he now lashes her to a lightning-rod during a thunderstorm and awaits a fortuitous strike.

36. No longer content with whipping, this libertine

makes his victim bend over then rams a gun-muzzle up her arsehole; the bullet destroys her entrails.

37. Bullwhipping a nude slut's entire body no longer suffices; he now breaks her every bone upon a wheel, then strangles her to death.

38. The libertine who would snatch a woman from decapitation at the last minute, now lets the blade fall true; he chases after the severed head, showering spunk in its eyes as it rolls away.

39. Instead of scarring a whore's skin, he flays it off and throws their raw bodies into dungeons carpeted in salt.

40. This libertine, who used to whip a pregnant woman's belly, now engineers an enormous rock to fall on it, pulping woman and embryo at one fell stroke.

41. As a young man, this libertine would discharge at the sight of a maiden's bare neck, which he would caress and squeeze somewhat. Now, he must impale girls' throats with a silver hatpin; they die instantly.

42. Formerly fond of singeing whores with a small candle, he now hurls them headfirst into a roaring furnace where they are incinerated in seconds. He wanks over the glowing ashes.

43. Once happy to prick women's arses with a pin, he now stabs them repeatedly through the heart with an icepick.

44. This libertine used to burn gunpowder in a slut's

cunt; this no longer suffices, and he insists on binding his victim to a sky-rocket. The fuse is ignited, the rocket blasts off, then plummets to earth with the girl still attached.

45. He used to pile gunpowder on a whore's body, but now wedges artillery cartridges in every orifice; they detonate simultaneously, blowing her limbs in all directions.

46. This libertine used to place an emetic in his victim's food; now he sprinkles a deadly powder onto flowers, the girl inhales, and dies with her entrails hanging out of her arse.

47. This libertine was in his youth a whipper of women's throats and breasts; now he is content with nothing less than a crowbar driven through their neck with demonic force.

48. He once lashed a slut soundly for farting; now his special passion requires a whore to enter the room, then shit loudly as she curtsies. He scolds her and, brandishing a bullwhip, chases her up to the attic. One of the ladder's rungs has been sawn through; it snaps, and she plunges into a vat of boiling oil where she perishes hideously.

49. This libertine, who has always specialised in unlubricated sodomy, now infects his wives' rectums with a deadly venereal disease; he has already dispatched twenty-two brides. They must all be virgins; nor does he ever stray from the anal path.

50. A well-known sodomist invites several friends to a poisoned banquet; with each successive course, more are

struck down with fatal stomach cramps. He plunges his cock into the liquid shit that pours from their arseholes.

51. Another demented buggerer distributes poisoned food to the poor, then rams his cock into the filthy corpses.

52. This libertine is not only a sodomist of international repute, but a powerful alchemist; he manufactures a drug which, spread about liberally, kills whosoever inhales it. He buggers the corpses.

53. He employs another drug which kills after weeks of agony. No doctor can cure it, and the libertine makes a point of visiting his victims on their death bed.

54. This libertine, a merciless sodomiser, employs a drug which induces death-like sleep. His victims are nailed in coffins and buried, shortly after which they revive. The libertine waits by the grave, placing his ear to the soil to hear a scream; if he does, it suffices to make him discharge over the gravestone. He has killed most of his family this way.

55. He is also fond of attending friends' dinner parties and there poisoning the most beloved friends or relatives of his host; he makes sure they die slowly and in agony.

56. This libertine, who once adored to lick sluts' tits, now has his revenge: he poisons infants being suckled by their mothers.

57. As a young man, this libertine would give a whore a milk enema, then suck it out of her arsehole; now, he pumps her arse full of toxic drugs which cause her spasms

and painful death.

58. This libertine is a pyromaniac, and will only set fire to poorhouses; he discharges to the sound of thirty children's bones roasting.

59. Another lusts after women who have died in child-birth; he administers poison to the infant and caresses both corpses.

60. If a woman gives birth and survives, his passion is to murder the child before her eyes the minute it leaves the womb; he does so while pretending to caress it.

61. The previous three libertines have a common passion: they require a woman eight or nine months pregnant; all three fall upon her, carve open her belly, rip out the unborn child and burn it before her eyes. Moreover, in the infant's place they ram a package of quicksilver and sulphur, which they also set on fire before sewing the belly up again with cat gut. The libertines watch the mother die in hideous agonies while three nude serving girls suck the spunk from their cocks.

62. An arch deflowerer, this libertine has refined his operations in the following manner: he keeps a harem of sluts and breeds a great number of children by them; when his offspring reach the age of five or six, he shreds the girls' hymens and splits the boys' arses open. Then he throws them into a blazing oven.

63. The libertine who used to play hangman now hides his valuables in a wardrobe then claims he has been robbed. The servants are arrested and he strives to have

them publicly hanged; if successful, he watches the spectacle, if not, he locks them in a room and has them strangled to death. Either way, he wanks himself raw during the process.

64. A coprophile of yore, this libertine has now constructed a special privy at his house. He induces a nude whore to sit upon it; at once the seat collapses and she is plunged into a deep ditch filled with rancid shit, in which she drowns while he showers her disappearing head with spunk.

65. The libertine who plays pranks with step-ladders has now refined his passion as follows: he seats a whore upon a trestle on the edge of a deep, water-filled ditch, and lights a bonfire under her arse; on the opposite wall is a ladder which seems to offer escape. To reach the ladder she must cross the moat. If she hesitates too long, she will roast; yet, as she cannot swim, she will probably drown if she enters the water. Invariably, his victim chooses the latter option. If she drowns, as frequently happens, the game is over; should she make it to the ladder, he ensures that a rung near the top is sawn through so that it breaks beneath her, and she is plunged into a hole disguised by a thin layer of soil. The hole is deep and contains a bed of red-hot coals, upon which she is grilled alive. The libertine wanks himself continuously throughout this drama, and discharges like a stallion at the moment of whichever form of death is the result.

66. A renowned arse-maniac procures the prettiest available girl of sixteen, and buggers her like a devil. Approaching his orgasm, he releases a hidden spring by which a machine furnished with jagged steel teeth fastens

its jaws about the girl's bare neck. The machine then begins to saw her head off while the libertine completes his discharge, which always takes a very long time.

67. This libertine declares his love for a girl and invites her out upon the lake in a small boat; the boat springs a leak, sinks, and she drowns. If she is afraid of water, he leads her out onto a high balcony; she leans upon the railing, which he has tampered with, and plummets to her death below.

68. While a mere apprentice in debauch, this libertine was content to whip and bugger his concubines; now, as a refined roué, he has the following habit: first, he lures his victim into a room; a trap-door opens beneath her and she plunges into the cellar where he awaits her. He falls upon her as she lies dazed, whips and buggers her, then plunges a knife into her tits, her cunt, and her arsehole. He then hurls her into another cellar already piled with rotting corpses, and rolls a heavy boulder over the opening. He is careful to administer non-fatal stabs, as he wants her to die slowly among the putrid bodies while he discharges to the sound of her wails.

69. This libertine has a whore sit astride an unbroken horse; the horse gallops away, bucking and battering her cunt to bits, throws her off and drags her screaming along a rocky path, then pitches her over a precipice.

70. A pyromaniac indulges the following passion: he marries a girl and ushers her to the conjugal bed; when she gets in, it collapses and drops her into a brazier of fiery coals. She manages to scramble out, but the libertine is at hand and drives her back into the inferno with a pitchfork.

71. Tired of torching poorhouses, this libertine now lures beggars out of them and invites them to dine at his own home. He ties up and buggers his guests, then breaks their backs and leaves them to rot in the dungeons.

72. As a young man, this libertine loved nothing more than to shove a nude slut headfirst into a dung-heap and then bugger her till her arse bled. Now, he has devised a more sophisticated game. He allows a girl to sleep in a chamber she is familiar with, whose window she knows to be close to the ground; opium is administered, and while she is stupefied he moves her to an identical room at the very top of his château. Later that night the libertine bursts into the chamber, terrifying her with a terrible racket and warning she is about to be murdered. She leaps from the window, expecting a short drop to the ground, and plummets onto the rocks far below. Her brains are dashed out, her entrails spray out of her cunt, but no-one has laid a finger on her.

73. Once content with administering twenty lashes, this libertine now thrashes a whore with a steel-tipped whip which removes a pea-sized lump of flesh at each stroke; he continues without respite, for several days, until her bones are stripped of meat.

74. A former blood-letter now relieves his victims of half a pint at a go; he and his cronies drink it, wanking as the donor dies.

75. Once content to stick a whore's arse with pins, this libertine now slashes her body all over with a dagger. The wounds are left untreated, and grow gangrenous. His accomplice, a renowned whipsman, quietly and slowly

saws off all four limbs, one after another.

76. This libertine loves above all to be horsewhipped for four hours; his second passion is to place a little girl in the hands of his giant servant, who holds her headfirst over a brazier. The victims, all virgins, are very slowly cooked.

77. This libertine, once content with searing a whore's tits and arse with matches, now manufactures his own pointed and sulphur-tipped slivers, which he plants all over her body, driving them in to the hilt. Then he ignites them one by one, and watches her go up like a firework.

78. As a lad, this libertine loved to suck a maiden's mouth and gargle her saliva; now, he sticks a funnel down her throat and, day by day, pours in a drop of molten lead until her smoking belly and guts rip apart.

79. A former finger-twister, he now insists on breaking all a bitch's limbs, tearing out her tongue, gouging out her eyes, then leaving her to starve in a snakepit.

80. A renowned blasphemer now goes so far as to sodomise then crucify a beautiful youth, leaving him as food for the ravens.

81. This libertine is an inveterate sniffer and fucker of filthy whores' armpits. He now hangs a naked woman up by ropes tied under her arms, and every day pricks a fresh part of her body to attract flies. She is stretched, starved, stabbed and eaten alive.

82. An arse admirer devises a special tribute: he hires virgins and spends a whole week kissing, licking and

sucking their arseholes, eating every ounce of shit they discharge; then he hideously wounds them and hurls them into an underground chamber with enough food for three days, throwing away the key.

83. Bored with fucking young girls' mouths and arseholes, this libertine now rips out the heart from a live whore, then fucks the warm hole it recently occupied. He shoves the heart back in amidst the blood and spunk, sews her up, and retires to his study.

84. A skilled whipper has mastered the art of gently removing every inch of flesh from a trollop's bones; he then sucks out the marrow through a steel tube and replaces it with molten lead.

85. By means of an ingenious device, a former sodomist now chops girls into exactly one thousand pieces.

86. This libertine, bored with deflowering maidens, now prefers to impale a girl's cunt with the point of a pick-axe. As she sits there, as if astride a horse, he affixes a cannonball to each ankle. The weight pulls her further and further onto the pick, killing her slowly and agonizingly.

87. The whipper flays three layers of skin from a nun, then douses the raw fourth with sulphuric acid.

88. Once happy to lop off the odd finger, this libertine now likes to pinch a whore's flesh with hot tongs, cut off the flesh with rusty scissors, then cauterize the wound with a firebrand. He may spend four of five days thus whittling the girl away, and she normally dies before the experiment is complete.

89. This libertine slices off a girl's tits and buttocks, grills and eats them, and covers her wounds with acid-soaked plasters which violently but slowly burn her to death. All the while she must join him in dining on her own flesh.

90. An arse-maniac, jaded by his former antics, now cooks his victims in a boiling cauldron. At least they die virgins.

91. Others are not so lucky; he buggers them brutally, for old time's sake, then roasts them on a revolving spit.

92. Another libertine used to enjoy watching girls and boys buggered by lackeys chosen for their enormous cocks; now he prefers to impale a girl himself and watch her slowly die with a spear up her cunt.

93. He ties other women to large wheels, then sets them rolling down the mountainside to a gory death.

94. This libertine used to like scarring girls' buttocks; now he bends four saplings, lashes a girl to them by all four limbs, then releases the trees so that his victim is torn into four pieces.

95. Bored with the lash, this libertine suspends his victims to a machine which lowers them into a furnace then quickly pulls them out; the process is repeated until they burn to a crisp.

96. This libertine used to snuff candles out on a whore's skin; now, he coats her from head to toe in sulphur and uses her as a human torch.

97. A seasoned sodomist, this libertine rips the intestines out of a young boy's arse, does the same to a girl, then inserts one's guts into the other and sews them up with wire. He watches, wanking, as they perish.

98. The libertine who used to inflict mild burns now shaves his victim from head to foot, marinades him in spunk and roasts him on a griddle, turning him over again and again.

99. This libertine places a woman so that the sharp point of a pole sticks up her arsehole; she is suspended over it by four slender cords. He laughs like a madman at her suffering, soiling his breeks, as she waits for the cords to snap.

100. A libertine who used to enjoy gouging small lumps of flesh from a whore's rump is now a fully-fledged butcher; he sandwiches a syphilitic trollop between two heavy planks and carefully saws through the lot.

101. This libertine, an inveterate buggerer of both boys and girls, fetches in a brother and sister; he declares to the brother that he is about to kill him, and shows him the terrible torture devices he proposes to use. However, he continues, the boy may save his own skin if he fucks and strangles his sister without further ado. The boy agrees and, while he fucks his sister, the libertine buggers them both in turn. Finally the brother, in order to save his life, wrings the life from the sister; at the moment she dies, the pair of them plunge through a set of trap doors into a huge charcoal furnace, where the libertine watches them be consumed by the flames.

102. He compels a father to fuck his own daughter while he watches; next, the father must hold down the girl while the libertine buggers her with arse-splitting thrusts. He then informs the man that his daughter must die, and gives him the following choice: either the man must strangle her himself; or the libertine will do the job, which will involve hideous tortures, while the father watches. The father invariably elects to kill her himself, and prepares a noose of black silk. At this point he is seized by the libertine's henchmen, trussed up, and made to witness his daughter being flayed alive and rolled on a bed of nails. Then the girl is cast into a brazier and the father strangled; this, says the libertine, is punishment for being so keen to choke the life out of his own children, which is barbaric. His corpse is dumped in the same brazier.

103. One of the great arse-whippers of all time plays a game with a mother and daughter; he tells the girl that her mother will be executed lest she, the daughter, sacrifice both her hands. She agrees, and her hands are severed at the wrist. Next, she is made to stand on a stool; a noose suspended from the ceiling is slipped over her neck. Another rope runs from the stool into the next room, and the mother is made to hold the end. She is ordered to tug the rope; not knowing what the result may be, she obeys. The libertine then leads her to the adjoining room to survey her handiwork and, at the moment of her most grievous distress, chops off her head with a sabre.

104. A mother and son are required for the next game; the libertine informs the woman that he is about to kill her, but will spare her if she murders her son. If she refuses, he slits the boy's throat before her eyes in any case; if she consents, which is rare, he ties her to her son's corpse and

leaves her to ponder as she starves to death.

105. This libertine, who prizes incest above all else, has devised a game for two sisters. He first buggers the pair of them, then ties them to an ingenious machine. Each girl has a knife in her hand; a hidden spring sets the machine in motion and they are flung towards each other at great speed. They simultaneously stab each other through the heart.

106. Another game involves a mother and her four children; they are locked up in a room, and he observes them through a small barred window. He starves them to death over a period of two or three weeks, keenly watching the mother's dilemma; he and his cronies lay wagers as to which child she will devour first.

107. His *pièce de résistance* requires a mother and daughter, both heavily pregnant. They are strapped to a pair of huge steel plates, one above and facing the other; the machine starts and the jaws of this vise snap shut with great power and speed, grinding both women and their unborn infants to pulp.

108. A well-known sodomist creates the following diversion: he convenes a mistress and her lover, who allow him to bugger them both in return for great favours. He then takes the lover to his study and informs him that the woman's husband, the one person standing between him and happiness, is asleep in the next room; the libertine has contrived to put him at the lover's mercy. He shows the lover to a dimly lit chamber and hands him a dagger; greatly inflamed, the man springs on the sleeping form before him and shreds it with a hundred stab-wounds. The

libertine illuminates the room; the lover sees that he has in fact killed his mistress. If he fails to kill himself in despair, the libertine obliges with a pistol-shot through the head; he has rid the world of two idiots.

109. This libertine buggers a lad then, at the point of orgasm, replaces his cock with the muzzle of a loaded musket. He pulls the trigger, and he and the gun discharge simultaneously.

110. This libertine forces a youth to witness his sweetheart being mutilated, then orders him to eat the flesh of her buttocks, breasts, and her heart. He is chained in a dungeon and, if he refuses to eat them, will starve to death. If the youth finally relents and eats his lover, the libertine gores him with a lance and leaves him to slowly bleed to death; if he abstains from the meal, his demise lasts even longer.

111. This libertine tears off a youth's testicles and shortly afterwards serves them up to him in a stew. He fills the boy's vacant scrotum with sulphur and quicksilver, ignites it, and proceeds to bugger him as he writhes in agony, compounding his suffering by burning him all over with matches then digging iron nails into the wounds.

112. He drives a long spike up his victim's arsehole, which emerges at the base of his spine and nails him to a pole. He then relaxes by watching the boy expire.

113. He puts a youth naked in the stocks and buggers him brutally; as he thrusts away, the youth's cranium is sheared off, the brains removed and replaced by molten lead.

114. He breaks a young boy on the rack, then nails him to a wheel where he is left to die; the wheel is slowly turned so as to expose the boy's buttocks. The libertine sets up his supper table directly beneath, and dines there each day until the victim has expired.

115. He flays the skin off a youth, impregnates the raw flesh with honey, and stakes him out beneath a bee-hive.

116. He slices off a lad's cock and nipples, nails one hand to a post and one foot to another, and leaves him to rot.

117. This libertine owns a lion. He arms a boy with a small stick and shoves him into the beast's cage. He wanks like a devil as the boy is mauled, bitten and chewed, only ejaculating when the last morsel is devoured.

118. He dresses one lad up as a horse and smears his arsehole with the cunt-cream of a mare. An excited stallion is led in; the libertine roars with laughter as the boy is penetrated and swiftly split in half.

119. This libertine places a boy in a machine which stretches him horribly, dislocating all his bones; the boy is then removed and crammed in a chest where his bones partly heal. The libertine then puts him through the machine again, back in the chest, and so on until the victim's death.

120. A young boy is strapped naked and spreadeagled on a table; the libertine instructs a beautiful young girl to wank him and suck him off for days until he is drained dry, starved, and dies with horrible convulsions.

121. In the space of one day, this libertine performs four operations on a young man; he removes a gallstone, trepans him, cuts out an ulcer from one eye, and another from the anus. A failed medical student, the libertine knows just enough of surgery to mess up each operation; he abandons his patient and watches him perish.

122. His next operation involves hacking off a boy's cock and balls, then hollowing out an artificial cunt with a red-hot branding iron; the iron makes the hole and cauterizes simultaneously. When the wound has cooled he fucks the boy's new orifice and strangles him to death as he discharges.

123. He abrades a lad's skin with a horse-comb, then rubs him with alcohol and sets him on fire; combs the charred flesh, rubs in more brandy, ignites it, and so on until no further care is necessary.

124. This libertine buggers a father whose two children must stand and watch; as he ejaculates, he plunges a knife into one child's heart and with his other hand snaps its sibling's neck.

125. This libertine used to content himself by lashing the bellies of pregnant whores. Now, he assembles six bitches whose term has gone eight months and ties them back to back, their bellies thrusting forward; he splits open the first with a razor, the second with dagger thrusts, gives a hundred kicks to the third, crushes the fourth with a hundred club-blows, burns the fifth, and applies an industrial rasp to the sixth. Those who survive he finishes off with a spiked truncheon.

126. This libertine assembles two nuns each week. He gives the first a choice: renounce God, and all religion, or die. But he has previously instructed his valet to whisper to her, warning her to say nothing or she shall surely be killed. Thus she remains mute; the libertine blows her brains out with a musket, crying out: "There's one for God!" The second nun, stunned by what she has witnessed, is quick to blaspheme and renounce God in the hope of saving her life; the libertine blows her head off as well: "And there's one for the Devil!"

127. An arch sodomist is fond of giving dances, but rigs the ballroom so that the ceiling collapses halfway through the evening, crushing all the revellers; he moves from city to city indulging this whim, and is only discovered after his fiftieth ball.

128. The compulsive abortionist has devised another scenario: first, he arranges three heavily pregnant women in an uncomfortable artistic pose; they must remain thus until all three give birth before his eyes. He then ties each infant to its mother's neck and leaves all six to starve. Each baby either dies of malnutrition, or is eaten by its parent. His other game involves two pregnant whores; both are blindfolded and then must give birth in his presence. The infants are placed side by side and each woman must recover her own offspring. If they choose the wrong child, he sends them on their way. If they are correct, he carves up the brats with a cavalry sword.

129. Another ploy involves imprisoning three pregnant whores in an iron cage; once they have whelped, he lights a roaring bonfire beneath the cage. The occupants hop and dance as the floor heats up, until it finally gives way and

all six plunge into the flames.

130. This libertine, an ardent arse-fucker, buggers a girl while her lover is forced to look on; he next buggers the lover while the girl must watch. Then he nails the two together, mouth to mouth, and leaves them to rot.

131. The libertine who loved to throw girls in a pond now does it eight at a time; he ensures they are poor swimmers and watches them thrash around; for good measure he has first amputated one of their legs. After a while he proffers an iron pike to cling onto, having heated it in a brazier. Some of the girls still grasp it, but he thrusts them away by bashing their heads with the severed limbs.

132. The libertine who liked to induce vomiting now has a larger aim: he poisons the streams, lakes and wells of an entire province, and revels as thousands die with horrible convulsions.

133. Formerly content with pricking a woman's skin, this libertine now has a pregnant slut sealed in a barrel whose interior is studded with razor-sharp nails; he then has the barrel rolled and dragged through the château grounds.

134. A renowned child-buggerer sodomises a group of girls and boys at the top of a tower, then stands outside where he has planted an array of sharpened steel rods. His henchmen pitch the infants out of the tower above; the libertine enjoys seeing them impaled a second time, and ejaculates only when he is soaked from head to toe in their blood.

135. The compulsive arsonist assembles six pregnant

women and bind them to bails of straw; these he sets afire and, should the women try to save themselves, he skewers them with a pitchfork and hurls them back into the blaze. When half-roasted, the floor beneath gives way and they plunge into a huge vat of boiling oil, which finishes them off.

136. This libertine, who hates the poor, assembles a group of beggars at a banquet table in his grounds. The earth beneath is strewn with land-mines and, as they begin to eat, the luckless wretches are blown to bits.

137. A notorious sodomist, seeking new ways to combine that crime with blasphemy, incest, murder, rape and adultery, first shits on a consecrated Host; he then rams this up his arse and has it tamped in by his son's cock; with the son's cock still in place he rapes his newly-wed daughter, beating the groom to her maidenhead, then tops it all off by pulverising his niece with a battering-ram.

138. Still aroused, he summons a mother and daughter to him; while violently buggering the mother he strangles her to death, turns her over and cunt-fucks her corpse, drooling on her belly like a madman. At the point of orgasm he butchers the daughter with a carving-knife, cutting off her tits, then buggers her dead arsehole for good measure. Raving, imagining they may yet be capable of more suffering, he hurls the cadavers into a furnace and wanks himself raw as they burn.

139. Once content with launching fireworks from a woman's arsehole, this libertine now binds two pregnant whores together into a ball and fires them skyward from a huge cannon.

140. This libertine used to amuse himself by picking open the scabs on a slut's tits; now, he gets two nude pregnant bitches in a room and has them fight each other with butcher knives. He threatens to shoot them if they do not comply. If they kill each other, his lust is sated; if not, he rushes into the arena and chops off the first one's head. He then disembowels the other and crams her dying cunt full of acid and red-hot shrapnel.

141. A libertine who used to whip pregnant women has reformed; he now likes to bind his pregnant victim to a wheel beneath which her mother is tied, immobile, in a chair. The mother's head is pulled back and her mouth wedged apart by an iron bit. The libertine slaughters the girl on the wheel, so that all the blood, shit and offal from her corpse drains into her mother's mouth, including the foetus.

142. A reformed arse-stabber now has more complex desires; first, he attaches a girl to a plank studded with sharp metal spikes and gives her a good fucking. Every thrust drives the nails into her arse-cheeks. He then turns her over and rams his cock up her arsehole, so her tits, belly and cunt may also be perforated. For the next phase of the operation, he lays a second wooden plank on top of her; the plank is also studded with rusty nails. By screws he brings the two planks together, and the victim is slowly crushed and stabbed to death.

143. A whipmaster stretches a heavily pregnant girl out on a table and nails her to it. First he drives red-hot nails through each eye, then one through her mouth, and another into each breast; then he sears her nipples and clitoris with a candle; then he half saws through her legs

and shatters her kneecaps; he finishes by hammering an enormous red-hot spike through her navel, which dispatches both the girl and her unborn child.

144. A sodomist has two girls brought to him, close friends, and binds them mouth to mouth. An excellent meal is set beside them, out of reach. He watches as, after several days of starvation, they begin to bite and eat each other's faces.

145. This libertine, who as a boy like to horsewhip pregnant women, now shuts six of them into a round cage of iron hoops so they all face each other. Little by little the hoops contract, and slowly all six women and their unborn children are flattened and crushed. Before tightening the hoops the libertine cut off a buttock and a breast from each and fashioned them into collars; these were nailed around their necks and they sport them like bloody ruffs.

146. He binds another pair of pregnant sluts, preferably two sisters, to the ends of two long poles; a machine drives the poles together so that the sluts collide with extreme force, and they suffer simultaneous miscarriages. The libertine sprays his spunk over the dying embryos.

147. His ultimate pleasure is in finding three pregnant women from the same family. These he likes to suspend over deadly hazards. The first hangs by her tongue over a deep well; the second, by her tits over a burning brazier; the third, by her hair over a forest of sharpened iron rods. Eventually, after hours of agony, they fall to their fate and the libertine wanks over their corpses.

148. The final libertine, the greatest of his kind, indulges

in an infernal caprice known as "the rites of Hell". He is forty years old, enormous in stature, and furnished with a huge cock some nine inches in girth and well over a foot long. He is exceedingly wealthy and powerful, aristocratic, and also utterly cruel, vicious and stone-hearted. He has a huge mansion on the outskirts of Paris which he maintains for the sole purpose of gratifying his evil lust.

He indulges his desires in a spacious room, sparsely furnished but padded everywhere, the floor covered in thick mattresses. Upon entering the room a single casement window is visible; this is the only entrance apart from the door. The window overlooks an underground cellar, twenty feet below the salon, which is also lined with mattresses to break the fall of any girls he may idly fling out. He requires fifteen girls for his entertainment, who must be aged between fifteen and seventeen, no more and no less. To find these girls he employs six procuresses in Paris and another dozen throughout the provinces; they are to spare no effort, no expense in finding him the most delectable specimens. Once recruited, the maidens are sent to a country convent over which he has absolute mastery, and there they ripen until he selects another fifteen of them for his debauch, which he performs once a fortnight.

That evening, before the ceremony commences, he scrutinizes every girl; the slightest defect warrants rejection, all his pupils must be models of beauty. Escorted by a procuress, they arrive at the house and are lodged in a room adjacent to the pleasure-salon. Here he strips them naked and proceeds to feel, fondle and examine each in turn, sucking their tongues before each is made to shit into his mouth. As if sampling fine wine, he tastes but does not swallow.

Having performed these preliminaries with deadly earnest, the libertine brands each accepted girl on the shoulder with a number; this shows the order in which he will receive them. That done, he retires to the salon and there remains, in silence and solitude, for an interval. No-one knows what he does during this time. Then he knocks; girl number one is cast into his lair, flung towards him violently by the procuress. He catches her in his arms, closes the door, then takes up a cat o'nine tails and gives her buttocks a fair whipping. After this he rubs pomade into her arsehole and sodomises her with his gigantic cock, penetrating with skill, but does not ejaculate. He withdraws his cock, still rock-hard, retrieves the cat and flails the girl's back, then both sides of her thighs; then he lays her down on her back and deflowers her cunt. Next, he thrashes her across the breasts, which he then seizes and starts to grind and knead with all his strength, which is considerable. When the breasts are well and truly bruised, he takes up an awl and stabs each of them six times.

Once all this has been accomplished, he opens the casement window and places the girl before it, standing to attention. He stands behind her and places around her throat a ribbon whose colour signifies the particular kind of torture he shrewdly judges most suitable for her; then, with an almighty kick up the arse, he sends her flying across the room. She crashes into the window sill, topples over it, and disappears into the cellar below.

In this fashion all fifteen girls pass through his hands, lose their front and rear maidenheads, are cat-whipped and pitched into the cellar; yet the libertine sheds nary a drop of spunk. The subterranean room is a dungeon, furnished with fifteen different kinds of torture device; a burly executioner, wearing the mask and emblems of a demon, and regaled in the colours of his particular speciality, presides over each fearful apparatus. As soon as the girl who sports the same colour ribbon lands in the pit, each executioner steps forward and drags her to his machine; nothing must happen until the fifteenth victim is claimed by her death-demon. Then the libertine, unspeakably aroused after fucking thirty orifices without discharge, his cock still rigid and flush with his belly, strides naked into the cellar. Everything is ready, and upon his signal the tortures commence simultaneously, amidst much screaming and grinding and din.

The first torture engine is a wheel upon which a girl is strapped; rotating constantly, the wheel interacts with an outer cog inset with razor blades which scratch, tear and cut the victim without respite. As the blades do not bite deep, the wounds are sufficiently superficial to ensure she takes a good few hours to bleed dry.

The second engine: the girl is suspended prostrate two inches above a red-hot iron plate which slowly cooks her.

The third: she is affixed by the waist to a mass of burning iron, then her limbs are twisted and horribly dislocated.

The fourth: the girl's four limbs are attached to coils which slowly move apart; eventually her arms and legs are ripped off and the trunk falls screaming into a brazier.

The fifth: a red-hot iron bell is lowered over her head, but does not touch her directly. Her head is slowly grilled, her brain slowly melts.

The sixth: she is chained inside an iron tub, the tub is filled with boiling oil.

The seventh: she is pinioned before a machine which, six times a minute, fires a dart into some new part of her body. The machine does not stop until she is entirely feathered, like a pin-cushion.

The eighth: her feet dangle over a furnace, then lead weights descend upon her head, pushing her ever further into the roaring oven.

The ninth: her executioner continually pricks her with a red-hot goad, meticulously working over every inch of skin until she is one giant blister.

The tenth: she is chained to a pillar beneath a large glass dome; twenty famished reptiles are released into the dome, and eat her alive.

The eleventh: she is hung on two slender cords; cannonballs are attached to her feet, and she eventually drops into a furnace.

The twelfth: a hook is driven through her mouth, she hangs there like a fish while boiling pitch is poured over her.

The thirteenth: the nerves are filleted from her flesh and tied to cords which extend them further; meanwhile burning nails are driven into her tits.

The fourteenth: she is alternately torn with pincers and whipped upon her cunt and arse with a lash whose steel tips are heated red hot, and from time to time her tits are striped with a burning iron rake.

The fifteenth: she is poisoned by a toxin which burns and scours her entrails, hurls her into terrible convulsions, and cause the most hideous screams; death ensues, but very slowly, and she is usually the last to perish.

As soon as the tortures commence, the libertine walks around the dungeon, contemplating each atrocity for fifteen minutes while swearing, blaspheming, and heaping the most hideous invectives upon the victims. When, towards the end of the ritual, his cock is finally fit to burst, he retires to a comfortable armchair whence he can observe the entire scenario; two of the demons whose subjects have already expired approach him, display their sweaty arseholes to him and wank him with all four fists.

The libertine spurts his hot spunk in pints over everything, bellowing and gibbering so loudly that his cries even drown out the shrieks of the surviving girls. His climax lasts for seven minutes, and then he abruptly quits the cellar. The executioners finish off with hammer blows those girls who have not yet died, all the corpses are buried in the grounds, and the rites of Hell are over till another fortnight passes.

THE LUSTS OF THE LIBERTINES
The Marquis De Sade

The Circle of Manias, the Circle of Excrement, the Circle of Blood; three gateways to a living Hell envisaged by the Marquis de Sade as he simmered in the bowels of the Bastille. An infernal zone where Libertines are free to pursue and execute their every caprice, no matter how depraved or inhuman.

Here, in a brand new, unexpurgated and explicit translation, are the 447 "complex, criminal and murderous lusts" of the Libertines as documented by de Sade in his accursed atrocity bible *The 120 Days Of Sodom;* a catalogue of debaucheries, cruelties and pathological perversions still unequalled in the annals of transgressive literature.

DUNGEON EVIDENCE: *Correct Sadist II*
Terence Sellers

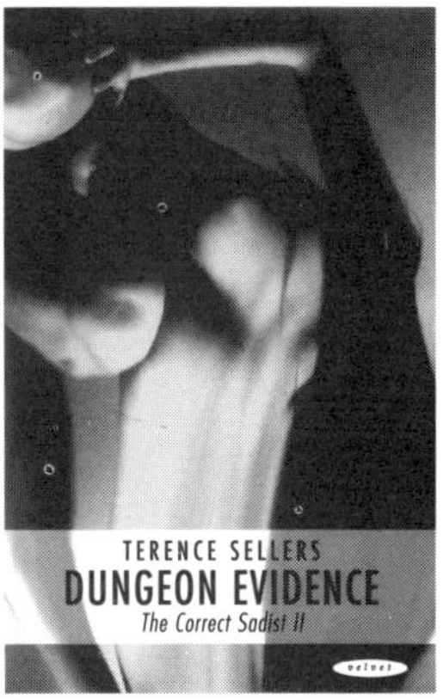

The Mistress Angel Stern presides without mercy over a New York dungeon where her slaves, the "morally insane" of modern society, obey her every whim and undergo any degradation she wills upon them.

In the closed confines of a torture zone, these paraphiliacs and sexual malcontents use her image as an object for their masturbatory depravities, craving her cruelty in an abyss of sadomasochism and bondage.

Here are the bizarre case histories, philosophies and psychopathologies of a dominatrix; a frank testament which reveals not only the drives which lead some to become slaves, but also the complex exchange of psychic energies involved in scenes of dominance and submission.

THE VELVET UNDERGROUND
Michael Leigh

Swingers and swappers, strippers and streetwalkers, sadists, masochists, and sexual mavericks of every persuasion; all are documented in this legendary exposé of the diseased underbelly of '60s American society.

The Velvet Underground is the ground-breaking sexological study that lent its name to the seminal New York rock'n'roll group, whose songs were to mirror its themes of depravity and social malaise.

Welcome to the sexual twilight zone, where the death orgies of Altamont and Helter Skelter are just a bull-whip's kiss away.

SISTER MIDNIGHT *Jeremy Reed*

The Marquis de Sade is dead – but his sister is alive and well, stalking the ruins of the château of La Coste where she reconstructs the apocalyptic orgies, tortures and blasphemies of her brother's reviled last will and testament, *The 120 Days Of Sodom.*

Castle freaks, killing gardens, lesbian love trysts on human furniture; these and countless other configurations of debauched carnality conspire and collude in a sundered, dream-like zone where the clock strikes eternal midnight.

Sister Midnight is the sequel to Jeremy Reed's erotic classic *The Pleasure Château,* a continued exploration of decadent extremes and sexual delirium in the tradition of de Sade, Sacher-Masoch and Apollinaire; a tribute to undying lust and the endless scope of human perversion.

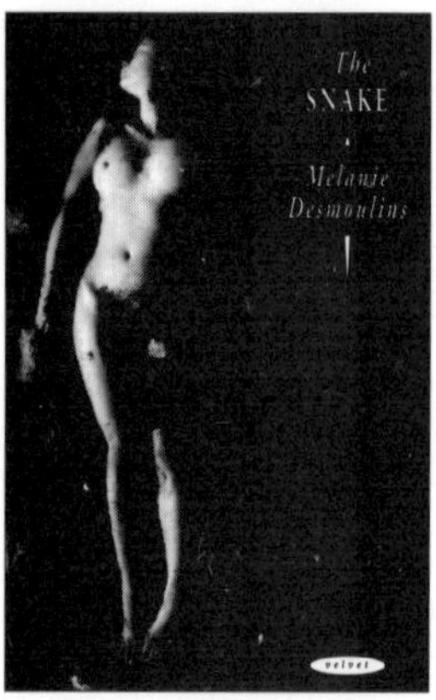

THE SNAKE *Melanie Desmoulins*

When Lucy, a sexually frustrated young widow, is mysteriously sent a plane ticket to Portugal, she takes a flight into erotic abandon which can only lead to death and damnation.

Soon seduced by both a debauched Englishwoman and her Portuguese husband, she sheds the skin of morality like a snake and begins to act out her darkest, uninhibited sexual desires. Increasingly depraved rituals of narcotics abuse, Satanism and sadomasochism – presided over by Bartolomeo, a Sade-like albino cult leader – eventually lead to the total disintegration of Lucy's ego.

At Bartolomeo's isolated villa, a shrine to pornographic art and literature, she finally enters the snake pit...

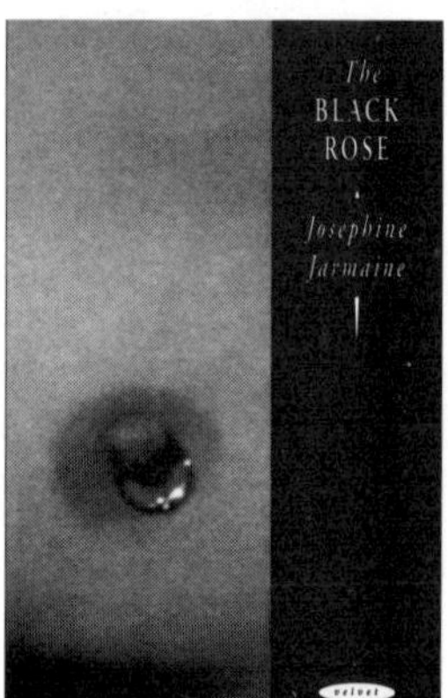

THE BLACK ROSE *Josephine Jarmaine*

Abducted to a mysterious French island, sixteen-year-old Rosamund finds herself at the mercy of the Duke and his four libidinous sons. She soon learns that her virginity must be sacrificed in order to breed the Black Rose, a rare flower whose aphrodisiac elixir will transform the world into a polysexual playground of orgiastic and orgasmic excess.

Rosamund's carnal initiation plunges her into a vortex of pain and pleasure, as she discovers that the Château Rose is a sensory realm where sadism, sapphism, sodomy, incest, bestiality, bondage and rampant fornication are a way of life.

The Black Rose is a stunning hybrid of decadence and explicit sexuality, a unique modern classic.

PHILOSOPHY IN THE BOUDOIR *The Marquis de Sade*

In the boudoir of a sequestered country house, a young virgin is ruthlessly schooled in evil. Indoctrinated by her amoral tutors in the ways of sexual perversion, fornication, murder, incest, atheism and complete self-gratification, she takes part with growing abandon in a series of violent erotic orgies which culminates with the flagellation and torture of her own mother – her final act of liberation.

Philosophy In The Boudoir is the most concise, representative text out of all the Marquis de Sade's works, containing his notorious doctrine of libertinage expounded in full, coupled with liberal doses of savage, unbridled eroticism, cruelty and violent sexuality. The renegade philosophies put forward here would later rank amongst the main cornerstones of André Breton's Surrealist manifesto.

THE SHE-DEVILS *Pierre Louÿs*

A mother and her three daughters...sharing their inexhaustible sexual favours between the same young man, each other, and anyone else who enters their web of depravity. From a chance encounter on the stairway with a voluptuous young girl, the narrator is drawn to become the plaything of four rapacious females, experiencing them all in various combinations of increasingly wild debauchery, until they one day vanish as mysteriously as they had appeared.

Described by Susan Sontag as one of the few works of the erotic imagination to deserve true literary status, *The She Devils (Trois Filles De Leur Mère)* remains Pierre Louÿs' most intense, claustrophobic work; a study of sexual obsession and mono-mania unsurpassed in its depictions of carnal excess, unbridled lust and limitless perversity.

THE PLEASURE CHATEAU *Jeremy Reed*

The story of Leanda, mistress of an opulent château, who tirelessly indulges her compulsion for sexual extremes, entertaining deviants, transsexuals and freaks in pursuit of the ultimate erotic experience. She is finally transported to a zone where sex transcends death, and existence becomes a never-ending orgy of the senses. The book also includes *Tales Of The Midget*, astonishing erotic adventures as related by a dwarf raconteur versed in decades of debauch.

Jeremy Reed, hailed as one of the greatest poets of his generation, has turned his exquisite imagination to producing this masterpiece of gothic erotica in the tradition of de Sade, Apollinaire and Sacher-Masoch, his tribute to the undying flame of human sexuality.

FLESH UNLIMITED *Guillaume Apollinaire*

The debauched aristocrat Mony Vibescu and a circle of fellow sybarites blaze a trail of uncontrollable lust, cruelty and depravity across the streets of Europe. A young man reminisces his sexual awakening at the hands of his aunt, his sister and their friends as he is irremedially corrupted in a season of carnal excess.

Flesh Unlimited is a compendium edition of *Les Onze Mille Verges* and *Les Mémoires d'Un Jeune Don Juan*, Apollinaire's two wild masterpieces of the explicit erotic imagination, works which compare with the best of the Marquis de Sade.

Presented in brand new translations by Alexis Lykiard (translator of Lautréamont's *Maldoror*), these are the original, complete and unexpurgated versions, with full introduction and notes.

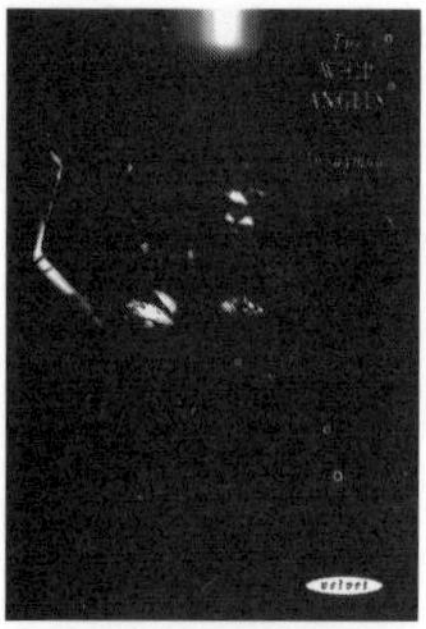

THE WHIP ANGELS *Anonymous*

Victoria's journal reveals her darkest secrets, her induction into a bizarre yet addictive sexual underground at the hands of her immoral, incestuous guardians. Behind the façade of everyday life seethes black leather mayhem, voluptuous eruptions of demonic angels from timeless torture zones, a midnight twist heralded by the bullwhip's crack and the bittersweet swipe of the cat.

Blazing with erotic excess and incandescent cruelty, *The Whip Angels* is a feast of dominance and submission, of corrupted innocence and tainted love. In the tradition of *The Story Of O* and *The Image*, this modern classic was written by an anonymous French authoress (believed to the wife of Georges Bataille) fully versed in the ways of whipcord and the dark delirium of those in both physical and spiritual bondage.

HOUSE OF PAIN *Pan Pantziarka*

When a young streetwalker is picked up by an enigmatic older woman, she finds herself launched on an odyssey of pleasure and pain beyond measure. Lost in a night world, thrown to the lusts of her anonymous captors, she must submit to their increasingly bizarre rituals of pain and degradation in order to embrace salvation.

House Of Pain is scorched earth erotica, an unprecedented glimpse of living Hell, the torments and raptures of a young woman abandoned to the throes of rage, violence and cruelty which feed the sexual impulse. Churches, hospitals, courtrooms, all become mere facets of the same unyielding edifice, a bedlam of desire and flesh in flame beneath the cold black sun of her own unlimited yearnings.

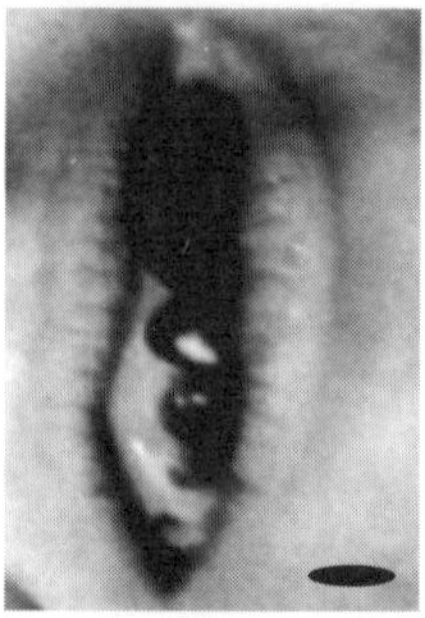

IRENE'S CUNT *Louis Aragon*

First published in France in 1928, *Le Con d'Irène ("Irene's Cunt")* is the last lost masterpiece of Surrealist Erotica. The author of this enigmatic and scandalous work is now known to be the great Surrealist Louis Aragon. Like Georges Bataille's *Story Of The Eye*, written the same year, *Irene's Cunt* is an intensely poetic account, the story of a man's torment when he becomes fixated upon the genitalia of an imaginary woman and is reduced to voyeuristically scoping 'her' erotic encounters.

In between describing various events in brothels and other sexual adventures, Aragon charts an inner monologue which is often reminiscent of Lautréamont, and of Artaud in its evocation of physical disgust as the dark correlative to spiritual illumination. This new edition features an exceptional and completely unexpurgated translation by Alexis Lykiard, and includes complete annotation and an illuminating introduction.

PSYCHOPATHIA SEXUALIS *Krafft-Ebing*

Lustmurder, necrophilia, pederasty, fetishism, bestiality, transvestism and transsexuality, rape and mutilation, sado-masochism, exhibitionism; all these and countless other psychosexual proclivities are detailed in the 238 case histories that make up Richard von Krafft-Ebing's legendary *Psychopathia Sexualis*. Long unavailable, this landmark text in the study of sexual mania and deviation is presented in a new, modern translation highlighting the cases chosen by Krafft-Ebing to appear in the 12th and final edition of the book, the culmination of his life's work compiled shortly before his death.

An essential reference book for those interested in the development of medical and psychiatric diagnosis of sexual derangement, the *Psychopathia Sexualis* will also prove a fascinating document to anyone drawn to the darker side of human sexuality and behaviour.

HEAT *Candice Black (editor)*

A compendium of erotic and sex-related photography, art and literature, featuring selections from past, present and future *Velvet* publications as well as material unique to this edition.

Photography: Richard Kern, Araki, Romain Slocombe, Peter Whitehead and Simon Starkwell, plus '70s porno cinema.

Writing: the Marquis de Sade, Terence Sellers, Lydia Lunch, Jeremy Reed, Peter Sotos, Krafft-Ebing and many others.

Graphic art: the complete 50-page version of Romain Slocombe's underground S/M classic *Prisoner Of The Red Army!*.

TORTURE GARDEN *David Wood (Editor)*

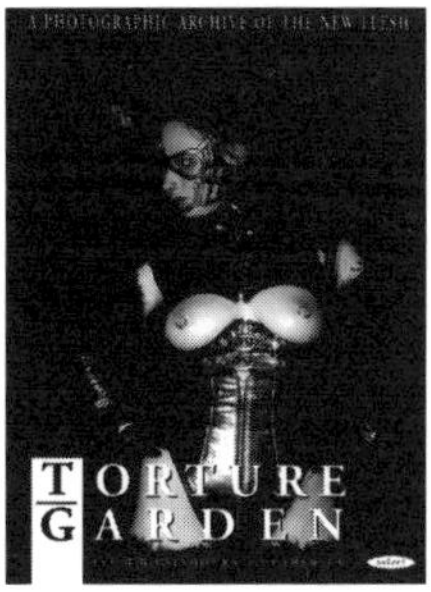

From Bodyshocks to Cybersex...A Photographic Archive of the New Flesh

A unique, definitive and breath-taking 5-year photographic record of Torture Garden – described by Marquis magazine as "the world's largest and probably most famous fetish club".

This deluxe book explores and celebrates the boundaries of the body and human sexuality with an extraordinary collection of images by the scene's two leading photographers, Jeremy Cadaver and Alan Sivroni.

An extensive collection of literary quotes juxtaposed with these stunning photographs helps create an anthropological, psychological and cultural backdrop to Torture Garden's position at the frontier of the fetish/body art phenomenon. The book includes some 350 original photographs, with over 50 colour plates.

BABY DOLL *Peter Whitehead*

1972 found Rolling Stones documentarist Peter Whitehead ensconced in a chateau in southern France with a teenage heiress model and a month's supply of film and psychedelic drugs. The startling results, never before published, are contained in *Baby Doll*, a beautiful yet disturbing visual diary of a lost four weeks spent in the pursuit of both physical and spiritual erotic extremes.

An uncensored, unflinching photographic journal of sexual metamorphosis and personality disintegration, *Baby Doll* is also a unique testament to Peter Whitehead's experimental vision, a forbidden legacy of an era simultaneously marked by its innocence and its license to explore previously uncharted areas of sexuality and psychic experimentation.

CITY OF THE BROKEN DOLLS *Romain Slocombe*

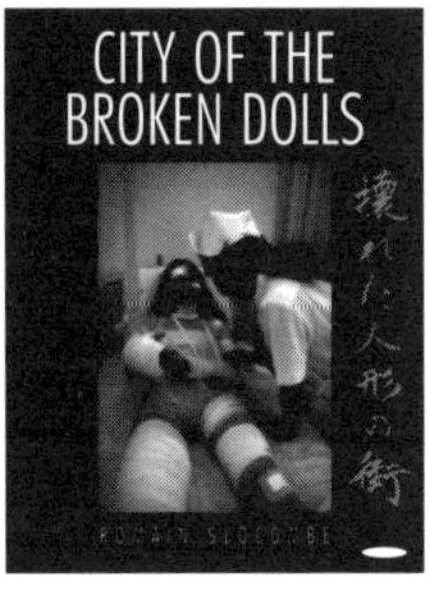

Tokyo metropolis. Both in hospital rooms and on the neon streets, beautiful young Japanese girls are photographed in plastercasts and bandages, victims of unknown traumas. These are the "broken dolls" of Romain Slocombe's Tokyo, a city seething with undercurrents of violent fantasy, fetishism and bondage.

Not since J G Ballard's legendary *Crash* have the erotic possibilities of trauma – real or imagined – been so vividly exposed. *City Of The Broken Dolls* is a provocative, often startling Photographic document of a previously unseen Tokyo, and of the girls whose bodies bear mute witness to the city's futuristic, erotic interface of sex and technology.

velvet

INFORMATION

You have just read a *Velvet* book
Published by:
Velvet Publications
83, Clerkenwell Road, London EC1R 5AR
Tel: 0171-430-9878 Fax: 0171-242-5527
E-mail: velvet@pussycat.demon.co.uk

Velvet publications should be available in all proper bookstores; please ask your local retailer to order from:

UK & Europe: Turnaround Distribution, Unit 3 Olympia Trading Estate, Coburg Road, Wood Green, London N22 6TZ
Tel: 0181-829-3000 Fax: 0181-881-5088

Italy: Apeiron Editoria & Distribuzione
Pizza Orazio Moroni 4
00060 Sant'Oresta (Roma)
Tel: 0761-579670
Fax: 0761-579737

USA: Subterranean Company, Box 160, 265 South 5th Street, Monroe, OR 97456
Tel: 541-847-5274 Fax: 541-847-6018

USA Non-booktrade: Xclusiv, 451 50th St, Brooklyn, NY 11220
Tel: 718-439-1271 Fax: 718-439-1272
Last Gasp, 777 Florida St, San Francisco, CA 94110
Tel: 415-824-6636 Fax: 415-824-1836
AK Distribution, PO Box 40682, San Francisco, CA 94140-0682
Tel: 415-864-0892 Fax: 415-864-0893

Canada: Marginal, Unit 102, 277 George Street, N. Peterborough, Ontario K9J 3G9
Tel/Fax: 705-745-2326

Japan: Tuttle-Shokai, 21-13 Seki 1-Chome, Tama-ku, Kawasaki, Kanagawa 214
Tel: 44-833-1924 Fax: 44-833-7559

A full catalogue is available on request.

ORDER FORM

(please photocopy if you do not wish to cut up your book)

TITLE *(please tick box)*	PRICE	QUANTITY	TITLE *(please tick box)*	PRICE	QUANTITY
☐ *The Lusts Of The Libertines*	£7.95		☐ *Flesh Unlimited*	£7.95	
☐ *Dungeon Evidence*	£9.95		☐ *The Whip Angels*	£4.95	
☐ *The Velvet Underground*	£7.95		☐ *House Of Pain*	£4.95	
☐ *Whiplash Castle*	£7.95		☐ *Irene's Cunt*	£7.95	
☐ *The Snake*	£7.95		☐ *Psychopathia Sexualis*	£9.95	
☐ *The Black Rose*	£7.95		☐ *Torture Garden*	£16.95	
☐ *Philosophy In The Boudoir*	£7.95		☐ *Baby Doll*	£12.95	
☐ *The She Devils*	£7.95		☐ *City Of The Broken Dolls*	£12.95	
☐ *The Pleasure Château*	£7.95		☐ *Heat*	£14.95	

Total Amount £__________ ☐ I enclose cheque/money order ☐ I wish to pay by ☐ Visa ☐ Mastercard

Card No: |_|_|_|_|_|_|_|_|_|_|_|_|_|_|_|_| Expiry__________

Signature__________________________ Date__________

Name__________________________

Address__________________________

__________________________ Telephone__________

Please add 10% to total price for postage & packing in UK (max. £5.00) 20% outside UK (max £10.00).
*Make cheques/money orders payable to **Velvet Publications** and send to 83 Clerkenwell Road, London EC1R 5AR (Sterling only)*

VELVET PUBLICATIONS